Murda Season 3

Lock Down Publications and Ca$h
Presents
Murda Season 3
A Novel by *Romell Tukes*

Murda Season 3

Lock Down Publications
P.O. Box 944
Stockbridge, Ga 30281
www.lockdownpublications.com

Copyright 2020 Romell Tukes
Murda Season 3

Lock Down Publications
Like our page on Facebook: Lock Down Publications @
www.facebook.com/lockdownpublications.ldp
Cover design and layout by: **Dynasty Cover Me**
Book interior design by: **Shawn Walker**
Edited by: **Leondra Williams**

Stay Connected with Us!

Text **LOCKDOWN** to 22828 to stay up-to-date with new releases, sneak peaks, contests and more...

Thank you!

Submission Guideline.

Submit the first three chapters of your completed manuscript to ldpsubmissions@gmail.com, subject line: Your book's title. The manuscript must be in a .doc file and sent as an attachment. Document should be in Times New Roman, double spaced and in size 12 font. Also, provide your synopsis and full contact information. If sending multiple submissions, they must each be in a separate email.

Have a story but no way to send it electronically? You can still submit to LDP/Ca$h Presents. Send in the first three chapters, written or typed, of your completed manuscript to:

LDP: Submissions Dept
P.O. Box 944
Stockbridge, Ga 30281

DO NOT send original manuscript. Must be a duplicate.

Provide your synopsis and a cover letter containing your full contact information.

Thanks for considering LDP and Ca$h Presents.

Romell Tukes

Chapter One
Nyack, NY

Murda was standing on his large terrace overlooking his nineteen acres on his beautiful 17,127 square feet mansion in Nyack, NY, forty minutes away from the city.

The mansion had its own guest house, which was mainly used for his large twenty-five-man security team. It had two outdoor pools, eight car garage, full basketball court, a sauna, a gym, and tennis court.

Inside was marble pattern floors, ten bedrooms, six bathrooms, three separate livings rooms, upstairs and down three levels, full-time house maids, a movie theater, basement bar area made for events and parties.

This was his and Jamika new home and they had a condo downtown in Manhattan in the Chelsea area.

Murda just got off the phone with a man name Zayid who he heard of when his father Web was alive. The man asked him if he could come to Abu Dhabi to have a sit down with him within a couple of weeks.

At first, he thought against because when his father went to Abu Dhabi, he never made it back because he was killed on the jet by Chelsea who sent him a postcard days later glorifying her work.

Out of respect, Murda asked if it would be cool for his goons to attend, and Zayid agreed.

Since the kidnapping of his newborn son, he hadn't been able to think right and every time he looked at Jamika, he saw the pain in her face, and he felt as if it was his fault.

Murda thought he killed Stacks that night. He was unaware Stack wore a vest that night and was rushed to the hospital within minutes because he was shot in the neck.

Luckily, he made it on time to the hospital so he wouldn't lose too much blood.

When Murda saw the letter written by the man he thought he killed, his heart almost stopped. Once he told Jamika what happened, she passed out but when she woke up, she told him the history with her and Stacks.

Murda had no clue she was dealing with Stacks before they met. It was crazy to him.

When she asked him about a man named Web, he told her that was his father. She was so shocked she couldn't talk. She started to piece everything up together and it all made sense to her.

Murda looked at a text he just got from Gunna telling him happy birthday. He turned twenty-four today.

He made plans to go out to eat with Jamika once she got off work. She still worked in White Plains, NY at the federal headquarters.

Before he could text his little brother back, Tookie was calling him.

"Yo, what's good, boy?"

"What's popping, blood? Happy birthday," Tookie said in the phone, sounding like he was driving somewhere.

"Thanks son. Good looking. I feel like an old nigga, word is bond," Murda stated.

"Nigga, please, I'm pushing thirty and a nigga looking fifty," Tookie said, laughing.

"That's a fact."

"Fuck outta here, nigga," Tookie replied laughing.

"Where you at, son? You and Gabby trying come out to eat tonight?"

"Sure, Gabby and Jamika are close now. Every time I turn around, they on FaceTime or Snapchat," Tookie stated.

"Aight cool. You in the hood?"

"Nah I'm about to go put some new flowers on lil bro's gravesite. I'm just pulling up. It's hella nice out today." Tookie got out of his car.

"I ain't been up here to see him yet," Murda said walking into his living room.

"I know, bro. It takes time, son."

"I be feeling like shit be my fault a little. You feel me?"

"You can't feel like that because everybody makes their own choices in life and to every action, there is a reaction," Tookie stated as he sneezed over the phone due to the pollen in the air.

"I'ma call you later. That's Jamika on the other line," Murda stated seeing another call coming in.

"I love you, fam."

"Love you too. Hit me later," Murda said hanging up as he accepted Jamika's call.

***

Brooklyn, NY

Tookie was walking up the hill, passing a couple holding each other hand crying for their recent loss.

Life had been in slow motion for him and Gabby, especially after beefing with Gabby's brother, Sergio, who was found murdered in his condo.

Tookie knew Gabby was the one when she killed a police officer just so they could get away from the scene after a shootout with Rafael's hitmen at the movie theater.

Before Gabby had their baby girl, Crystal, Tookie married her because Gabby feared having a baby out of wedlock. It wasn't how she planned to have a family.

Tookie and Gabby owned a pizza shop and a bar in Tarrytown, NY where they lived in a nice home with a fence, neighborhood watch, and police patrol.

Tookie gave the drug game up once he had a family, but he was still willing to ride or die for Murda and Gunna at a drop of a dime.

There was a new fresh set of pink flowers on YB's gravesite, which made Tookie mad because pink was a sign of disrespect. In Brooklyn, it was either red or white flowers people picked on their loved one graves unless they were babies.

He grabbed the flowers and tossed them into the bushes on the side of him. YB's grave was all the way in the back of the graveyard next to the bushes and wooded area.

Tookie was Muslim but he was also a big homie Blood member. He loved his den, though. He even convinced Gabby to become a Muslim woman and now she was full blown Muslim.

The two planned to pay a visit to Hajj soon in Mecca a place where Muslim's at least having to visit once in their lifetime.

Tookie said a silent prayer for his little brother and loved ones that weren't here today.

When he opened his eyes, he saw something he was too familiar with. A pistol to his face.

"Tookie, nice to finally meet you handsome." said Chelsea dressed in camouflage pants and a hoodie despite it being eighty-seven degrees.

"Who the fuck are you?" Tookie looking at the beautiful red head woman he never saw before.

"I'm your worst fucking nightmare."

"You don't look like chucky the bride to me," Tookie said making her laugh.

"Thank you, but I must say, you're sexy as hell and all them big muscles are about to go to waste. If I wasn't going to kill you, I would of love to fuck the shit of you and suck your dick all night," she said sadly.

"Sounds scary. You must be Chelsea."

"Here in your presence. It's been a while, but I'm back. The boss bitch is here to stay so I have to go. Murda is nex.t I'ma do him just like I did Web," she said before shooting him eleven times in his face, as his big wide muscular body collapsed on his brother's gravesite.

Chelsea snuck back off into the woods to her car parked across the street from the graveyard. She been following Tookie since he come in Brooklyn hours ago. She knew he was coming to visit YB, so it was perfect for her.

Murda Season 3

Chapter Two

Brooklyn, NY

Gunna listened to the sounds of Fabolous, one of his favorite rappers besides Jadakiss, as he hit the gas on his all red Bentley Flying Spur W12 S with black rims, peanut butter seats, and a sunroof.

He was on his way to Washington Heights to pay his connect a visit and talk about their next drop off.

Since Web was killed, Murda didn't have a plug so Gunna didn't have a plug, until he met a Dominican man in Dykeman one day name El Niño.

Gunna was now heavy in the dope game. He supplied Brooklyn and other borough's as well filling his brother shoes. Murda had a couple of businesses he opened until he was able to find a steady plug.

After Live was murdered, Gunna built a new team because the beef with the Mafia almost ended Murda and his career.

The recent news of Tookie's death shocked the city, and everybody wanted blood. His brother was taking it the worse and so was his little cousin, NH who was now Gunna's right hand man.

It was the beginning of summer and the streets of Washington Heights were filled with beautiful women, mostly Spanish women who looked like Cardi B and J-LO.

Gunna stopped at the light on Post St to see everybody looking at his new Bentley, thinking he was famous. When he got to Post and Academy, he parked behind a BMW X5 with tints and hopped out with his gun in his lower back.

It was a hot New York day as Gunna wore Balmain jeans, a Balmain t-shirt, and Giuseppe's shoes with his Audemor Piguet watch worth $212,500. Gunna rocked waves, clean cut, handsome, tall, brown skin and was a ladies man.

He saw a couple of Dominican's sitting out front playing cards, but watching his every move, as he walked between two buildings, and down some stairs leading into a dirty alley that lead to the back.

Once all the way in the back, he saw El-Niño playing chess with another older Spanish man as they sat on milk crates, both watching the chess board.

"One second, Gunna. It's about over for him anyway," El-Niño said in his strong Spanish accent as he made two more moves and the game was over. The older Spanish man said something in Spanish and walked out front, leaving El-Niño laughing.

"Have a seat, Gunna. Let's get a game in. I'll let you redeem yourself from last time."

"If you say so," Gunna said sitting down placing the pieces in their correct place as he took white and made the first move.

***

El-Niño Gomez was from La Romana, Dominican Republic, but moved to Washington Heights, NY for his daughter and to gain control of the drug trade.

There were many kingpins in the Heights but El- Niño had the best uncut, purest product in the city.

He was sixty years old and very wise. All of his gray hairs told a story. He came from poverty. Now he was a millionaire with three homes in DR, two in New York, two Spanish corner stores, and a restaurant.

When he saw Gunna two years ago in his restaurant, he liked his style, and he could tell by his fancy car and jewelry that he wasn't a college kid. There first conversation was about worldly matters, then poverty in the urban communities and after that it was about money, which led to him telling Gunna that he was the man that could help his money issues.

Gunna was his only black client and he bought more keys than all of his other clients put together.

***

Minutes later

El-Niño's face was screwed because Gunna had one move left and the game would be checkmate. Niño took losing serious as if it was based on a man's strength and honor.

"Checkmate," Gunna said trapping off his king with his Queen and Bishop.

"Wow, good game my friend. I must admit, I'm highly surprised. This is my first time losing in years. Maybe I'm getting old," Niño stated with a fake laugh.

"You win some, you lose some."

"Yes, but how can I help today. I'm sure you're aware your shipment arrives within hours," Niño said leaning back on to the wall.

"I know but I've came to speak to you about the prices."

"Did we miscalculate something?"

"No, it's just I've been doing good business with you for a while now and you're still taxing me. I'm paying twenty- seven for a key and I'm buying by the boat load." Gunna said giving his sagaciousness insight on Niño taxing him.

Gunna already got word Niño's other clients were getting keys for as low as twenty-two grand.

"One thousand to fifteen hundred keys once a month is not a boat load, my friend" Niño stated sarcastically.

"Just work with me, not against me."

"I'm sorry Gunna, but business is business," Niño said looking up to make sure all of his shooters were in place.

"Ok I just had to ask, but I will have your money to you within days, some way," Gunna said standing to leave.

"Thank you, but I'm sure understand my position."

"Yeah no doubt," Gunna said walking out front as two Latino men passed him going to see Niño.

Gunna had a feeling this was going to happen, so he had to pull out his wild card.

***

Brooklyn, NY

Ariana was walking through the King Plaza mall doing some shopping for the summer. She was glad the long, cold winter was over, especially since she was stuck in the house half of the time with the flu.

As she walked into the Dolce & Gabbana store, males couldn't help but stare at her high yellow features and beautiful face. Everybody would call her ma or beautiful, while trying to get her attention, but it only made her walk faster.

Life was ok for Ariana. She was now living in Brooklyn in an apartment just to be close to her brother she recently met before her father was murdered.

After being kidnapped by Elena, and thankfully escaping, she came to New York to find her brother, Murda, who found her.

Ariana was out of the military now and she was focused on running her flower bouquet in downtown Brooklyn. She was loving her new life. It was quiet, peaceful, and she didn't have to worry about killing nobody as she had to do overseas to protect her life.

Her relationship with her brother, Murda was great. He bought her the bouquet, a nice condo, and a new Lexus GS F/LC 500 coupe, all red and hooked up.

The two had sister and brother date night. It was crazy to her how the two of them were just alike in so many ways.

Ariana's mom Katherine just left town from visiting her since she lived in Atlanta. Since she was running her hair salons, the two never got to see each other so she would come up for a week every six months.

She saw some nice D&G dresses that would fit her perfectly as she went to try them on. Lately, she been in the gym heavy working on her squats and lunges, focusing on a bigger ass.

After forty minutes of shopping and spending $18,527, she was done for the day, so she carried her bags to the car ignoring the crew of men whistling at he,r unaware she was a cold-blooded killer.

Ariana went home took a bubble bath with candles and re-laxed thinking about the life she missed deep down. In her heart, killing was the only thing that brought joy to her so without it she truly felt empty.

Chapter Three

White Plains, NY

"Jamika, can you push these names in the database and tell me what pops up? I need their last place of residents and contacts of all their loved ones," her boss said dropping off a small stack of papers.

Ever since Jamika's daughter was kidnapped two years ago at the hospital by Stacks, she felt a piece of her was gone.

Her relationship with Murda was stronger than ever since the situation happened. He was there for her 100%.

She was still at her job working as an F.B.I agent. Only few people knew about her child being kidnapped, because it made world news years ago.

Jamika couldn't believe her ex-boyfriend Stacks was back from the dead and stole her baby to get back at Murda for trying to kill him.

Murda stopped selling drugs and opened a couple of businesses, which made it easy for Jamika to come back to work a year later. Jamika saw it was time for her lunch break, so she planned to go to Subway down the street. She had a rookie partner, who was fresh from college named Ronny. He was a smart white kid.

Ronny heard what happened to her last partner Agent Lopez who was found murdered with his wife and was a little scared to work with her.

"Hi, Jamika. Where you going?" Ronny asked walking out the restroom to see Jamika at the elevator looking sexy in a Gucci suit and heels.

"Lunch. You want to come?" she said looking at the nerdy kid.

"I just ate some salad, but thank you," he said in his tight suit.

"Okay," Jamika replied shaking her head because he was extra weird, she thought to herself as she got in the elevator.

***

Manhattan, NY

Chelsea was walking down the hotel hallway on her way to the conference room for her meeting with the other mob families.

Since becoming the "Godmother" of the Mafia, she been on her high horse. Killing Tookie was only the beginning of the mayhem she was about to cause in New York to destroy Web's bloodline and legacy.

After she lost her children and heart to the hands of a man who was her Godfather, her heart turned cold.

Once she killed her husband, Chris who was also the brother of Web, her father was next so she could take his throne and empire as the Mafia's boss bitch.

She knew killing Web on his jet wasn't smart, but it was all part of her plan.

Today, she called a meeting with the three biggest Mob families in the Tri-state to declare war.

Her guards opened the French doors for her as she stepped in the room wearing a beautiful white Valentino Houte Couture dress with heels.

"Welcome families," she said welcoming everybody in the room as she looked around the medium sized tables to see an older gentlemen in a gray suit, which was Fernando Swonepoel, the middle aged handsome Italian man named Silvio Janeiro and then she looked at the blonde head beauty who looked like a model instead of a crime boss.

"I'ma make this short and sweet. We're about to go face to face with a very dangerous family out here in Brooklyn," Chelsea stated looking at the three heads at the table.

"If I may ask, who and why?" Fernando asked looking at her as if she was crazy because his family hadn't been to war since the 90's with other mob families.

"His name is Murda. He is the son of Web. I killed Web years ago," Chelsea stated brushing her red hair back.

"I believe I've heard of him," Silvio stated.

"Yeah me too. I heard they're dangerous," Susanna said fixing her dress top as her big nice breast were about to pop out.

"They're not to be slept on, but trust me, together we can clean them up with ease," Chelsea stated seriously.

"What is the reason and benefits behind this?" Fernando asked as he saw Chelsea's face frown in anger.

"Why the fuck do you always have so many questions?" Chelsea replied rudely.

"Because I just want to know what we're getting ourselves and families into."

"Does it matter? We're the Mafia. We do as we please unlike Joe Da Don and Sergio."

"Aight," Fernando stated not trying to argue with the crazy bitch.

"Thanks for coming out. I'll send you all the info you will need on our ops," Chelsea walking out smiling strutting her nice round ass and curves.

***

Washington Heights, NY

Niño pulled up in the passenger seat of his Rolls Royce Phantom black on black with his bodyguard driving. He was at one of his stash apartments on Court St so he could pick up some money from his workers.

Niño's driver hopped out and opened the door for his boss as Niño hopped out in a suit looking up and down the dark block.

"Let me this shit quick," Niño said, walking up the stairs into the brick building to the third floor.

***

NH was in the passenger seat of a black Suburban truck with goons watching Niño's every move closely.

NH was Gunna's right hand man from Flatbush, Brooklyn. He controlled the drug traffic on his side of BK while Gunna controlled downtown and East New York sections.

He was cripping heavy and had a mean team of Crips willing to die for him at any second. At twenty-years-old, he was still living life, but now with a lot of money thanks to Gunna. He met Gunna through Live when he and Live were in Rikers together

The women loved him. He was tall, lean, light skin, waves in his head, green eyes, tattoo's, fly, cocky, and he had a big bag.

"I think it's time," NH said grabbing his Draco as he hopped out the truck with four Crips behind him.

The hallway doors were both unlocked as they entered the building to see an elevator and stairwell door.

"Come on," NH said taking the stairway. As soon as he made it to the first level, he heard someone talking on the in Spanish the next flight up.

NH placed a finger on his lips and slowly crept up the stairs with his weapon drawn and his team behind him

When he made it to the top level, he saw a big Spanish man talking on the phone with his back turned towards the stairwell.

"Don't fucking move, papi. Take me into the apartment Niño went into," NH said with his Draco pointed at the back of his head.

"Ok papi, easy, easy, please," the man said leading them in the bright hallway. "He's in 3B."

"Knock on the door. No funny shit, bro," NH said standing on the side of the door.

"What?"

"Knock muthafucker," NH yelled as the man knocked twice with a nervous look. Seconds later, a man opened the door and said something in Spanish. The man had cold feet as if he was scared to come inside

Bloc!
Bloc!
Bloc!
Bloc!

Bloc!
Bloc!
NH shot the man in the head while standing outside the door then he hit the Spanish man sitting in the doorway three times in his chest.

Niño and his two soldiers popped out of the back with assault rifles, firing shots as NH took cover as one of his men got hit back.

"Fuck you! Smell, take my left, Boy and Jody cover me, cuz," NH said a bullet took chunks out the walls.

Bloc!
Bloc!
Bloc!
BOOM!
BOOM!
BOOM!
NH took out one of Niño's man as he posted on the wal,l watching Smell go toe to toe with Niño's last shooter using him as a decoy.

Tat!
Tat!
Tat!
Tat!
Tat!
Tat!
Niño shot towards NH's head, yelling something in Spanish after NH shot him in his pelvis area, making him fall, while Smell shot his guard in the head.

"I should torture your bitch ass," NH said standing over Niño, kicking his SK to the side. "Empty this spot out take everything," NH told his crew as he saw his homie, V5 dead near the kitchen.

"You're a dead man," Niño said in pain, unable to breath.

"You need to find a new death theme. That's been used so many times." NH said before letting the Draco bullet rip his face in half. "Come on we gotta go" NH yelled as his crew came out with four duffle bags, the bags Niño came for. NH texted Gunna once in the truck letting him know everything was good and crisp.

Chapter Four

Abu Dhabi

Murda was in the back of a Porsche stretch limousine with six of his Brooklyn goons. Murda didn't roll with security as his father did. Instead, he handpicked niggas from his hood East New York to roll with him.

"Yo Murda this shit out here is a different type of ball game," Ja said looking at the tall glass buildings, fancy cars, beautiful women, desert heat, beaches with crystal clear water, and rich Arabian's.

"This shits aight, homie. We gotta pull up on a vacation out here one day," Murda stated as the limo went into an underground garage filled with foreign cars.

Murda didn't have a clue as to why Zayid wanted to see him. To make matters worse, his father came to Abu Dhabi and never made it back to New York.

"Gentlemen, the elevator awaits you all," the driver said as Murda saw two bodyguards dressed in suits waiting in the glass elevator for their boss' guest.

Once in the elevator, they rode to the penthouse suite in the most expensive complex in the city.

"This shit nice. They ain't got no shit like this in New York," Big Bug said looking out the glass elevator.

"Nigga, how you know? You've never been out of Brooklyn," Ja replied as Murda laughed.

When they all stepped off the elevator, everybody was in a loss of words because everything was gold, even the gold shiny floor.

"Murda. Which one of you men is Murda?" Zayid said walking from around the corner in a white Muslim garment with ten huge guards behind him.

"That will be me," Murda said stepping up in a red Tallia suit with a black tie.

23

"Your crew can go to my pod area. It's full of women and they can enjoy themselves while we talk business if that's ok with you?"

"Sure," Murda said giving his crew a nod.

"Ok follow me," Zayid said walking off with Ali behind him as his guard's led Murda's crew to the indoor pool area filled with women, food, and liquor as well as any drug of choice.

Inside of Zayid's living room was a home within itself with an expensive waterfall that was all gold in the middle of the floor, surrounded by Armani couches and two gold pianos.

"Would you like a drink?" Zayid said pouring himself a drink at his private glass bar near his large window where he could see the beautiful city.

"I don't drink."

"Good and thank you for coming out. I'm very sorry about your father but the night he was killed, he came from a meeting with me. Long story short, he told me if anything was to happen to him, then approach you with my helping hand," Zayid said now sitting down rubbing his big reddish Muslim beard.

"Helping hand?"

"Yes, my helping hand. Murda, I've been watching your father for years and he was a brilliant man. I've been watching you for a little while and you're not too far behind. I'm offering a share of my pie for a small fee."

"Is that right? As you know, all business isn't good business," Murda replied looking him in his eyes trying to find a hidden agenda.

"Correct but your business is only as strong as you and your morals, Murda. This is why I'm one of the biggest drug suppliers in the world." Zayid stated smoothly

"I'm not really in the game no more."

"True but your brother is and I'm willing to give you keys as low as ten grand a piece. Plus, the dope and coke is pure," Zayid said as Murda thought he was hearing shit.

"Hold up, so you're telling me you're willing to give me keys for ten bands each?"

"Yes."

"But you're losing money. Business is about profit."

"Yes, but I have too much, and I need someone of your speed to help me get rid of them," Zayid said getting up looking out his window.

"Ok I'll think about it."

"I'm sorry, Murda, but I need to know an answer before you leave. I'm a firm believer in treating my clients as if they're family," he said as Murda was in deep thought.

Murda been living a square life for two years. He missed the hustle and taking care of his people.

"Ok we have a deal but if you ever cross me…"

"It's no need for ideal threats," Zayid cut him off. We're on the same team now. You have my trust and honor just as I should have yours," Zayid said serious, looking Murda in his colorful eyes.

"Agreed"

"Good. Now that we're family, you have a big problem on your hands, Murda. I believe you was blindsided by your child being kidnapped. You were unable to see the threat lurking in your back yard."

"How did you know my son was kidnapped?"

"I know everything, and I have eyes everywhere. Just like I know who killed your father "

"What type of games are you playing?" Murda shouted getting upset.

"I had nothing to do with his death if that's what you were thinking. He was family. By the time I found out his plane was hijacked, it was too late. I wish he would've taken my jet as I recommended," Zayid said grabbing a folder from his dining room table.

"Who did it?"

"Here is everything you need to know about who you're up against and please don't let the pretty look fool you," Zayid said tossing a folder on the table as Murda opened it to see a beautiful white woman with long red hair.

"Chelsea. I think name sounds familiar."

"I'm sure it does," Zayid replied.

"Why would she kill my father?"

"Read it. She was married to your uncle before she killed him. She runs the mafia now since her father was killed. This bitch is vicious, Murda. Be smart. I'ma send you some help. My daughter she is built Ford tough as you Americans say.

"I can build an army in no time."

"I know, but please I insist."

"Aight, thank you for this."

"No problem. I wish I can help get your son back, but I have no clue who was behind that."

"You've done enough."

"Glad to help, but I'll be in town with you soon as far as our business, but just stay awoke. My daughter Zaby can handle herself. Trust me."

"Aight."

"Now let's go enjoy the evening," Zayid said leading him to his indoor pool area to see his crew fucking and sucking on bad Arabian bitches as if they were on a porn set.

Chapter Five

Mount Vernon, NY

"Damn bro, you gotta go get some air. You've been stuck to the couch for weeks, son," Black told his cousin as he just walked in the house from work at Wal-Mart.

"I just been putting some plans together youngin," Stacks said watching the world news.

"Aight, I'm about to call some bitches over. Mary's friend said she is trying see what's up with B. You know she like them chocolate niggas."

"Nah all them bitches want to do is smoke and drink a niggas shit up. You need to find a real woman and leave them basic thots alone," Stacks said getting up walking to his room to get dressed, so he could go for a walk.

Stacks been hiding out in Mount Vernon for nearly over three years after being shot by Murda and survived. He played the background until it was perfect timing.

He kept a close eye on Jamika and Murda. When he saw them fucking around, he wanted to pop up and kill them both. Luckily, he was able to keep cool and form a plan when he saw Jamika was pregnant.

Stacks was able to sneak into the hospital dressed like a doctor and steal their son, Andrew with ease. The baby was being watched by a babysitter in Brooklyn, safe and sound.

Stacks walked out the building in a Gucci hoodie, covering his dreads he recently grew to change his appearance. Stack made a few calls to some important people, so he could put his plan into motion and step one was reaching out to Elena, the Venezuelan cartel boss he had heard so much about.

***

Queens, NY

"Ugh! Ummm," Chelsea groaned loudly as she slowly grinded her ass up and down on the big black dick.

"Mmmm. You are dripping wet ma," Curt said. Curt was a young black man she met in a city bar hours ago and they kicked it off.

Curt then took her to a hotel room in Queens two blocks away from his hood. When he saw the bombshell thick, sexy redhead he had to have her, and she had the best pussy he ever had.

Curt fondled and sucked her nice firm breasts, while licking her pink nipples as she picked up the pace on his dick about to climax as he spread her ass cheeks.

"Ohhh I'm cumminggg," She screamed, feeling him in her stomach as her pussy muscle tightened around his nine-inch dick.

After she came on his dick like a waterfall, she climbed off. His dick was still hard, so she sucked him off slowly in a rhythm as he eased down her throat touching her tonsils.

"Fuck," Curt said as she spit his precum back on his dick and then sucked faster until he came in her mouth. She sucked all his cum out and went to spit in the toilet.

"Fuck me from behind," she demanded. Bending over, he saw her wide ass and pink pussy with a swollen clit. Curt started to fuck her from the back, grabbing her waist pumping his pole into her as her body jerked.

Her gasps filled the room as she climaxed twice, especially after he put her thumb in her butt. After they both came again, Curt was drained, which disappointed her because she wanted more.

"When I wake up, we can go again before I have to go home to my wife," Curt said with his handsome smile, kissing her on her cheeks.

"Wife?"

"Yeah I forgot to tell you, I'm married."

"Oh wow. Okay," Chelsea said with a smirk as he laid down and she went to the restroom to clean up. Minutes later, Chelsea got dressed in her pink Givenchy dress, that hugged her curves and breast.

"You ok? Where you going?" Curt turned around with his muscular defined body.

"I'm going the opposite way of where you're going," she said, confusing him as she pulled out a Glock 21 handgun and shot him five times in the head before leaving.

Her guards were waiting outside. They followed her around in the bar and when she went to the hotel in Curt's BMW M2 coupe.

**

Al Fuijayrah, United Arab Emirates

Khalifa was on the phone in his limo full of security guards. He was on his way to his private G6 jet to attend a meeting in Saudi Arabia with a powerful Mayor to discuss oil trades.

Khalifa was ten times richer than Bill Gates. He controlled a lot of Middle Eastern Oil. He was born into a Muslim royal family that was already rich from oil fields and pipelines they owned.

Months ago, he went into a business agreement with Zayid about some oil trades they planned to do but instead of keeping his word, he backed out and kept Zayid's two billion dollars.

Khalifa always felt as if he was untouchable and as if he could do whatever he pleased because he had money and power.

The limo was driving down a highway on the nice bright sunny day.

BOOM!

BOOM!

BOOM!

BOOM!

The bullets shattered the windows, taking out three of his guards with head shots.

Khalifa screamed as he looked back to see a motorcycle on his door side, causing him to duck as the window shattered hitting another guard.

"Go, go, go," Khalifa yelled to his driver, as he felt the tire go out as the limo spun off the rode into a ditch.

Khalifa was dizzy as his limo door flew open and the gunmen shot his last two guards and the driver behind his head.

"Please I have money. I…"

BOOM!

BOOM!

Khalifa was silenced by two rounds in his forehead as the gunmen wore a tight biker suit and helmet with long hair hanging out the helmet.

The shooter hopped back on the Honda C7VS new sports red motorcycle, speeding off popping wheelies.

***

Hours Later
Abu Dhabi

"Good job. I wish I could have killed him myself. He had the nerve to cross me and rob me at the same time, but thanks. I need you to do me a favor. I need you to go to the states, New York, I believe for a while and watch over some important people for me." Zayid asked his daughter who just came back from killing Khalifa.

"Father, I hate going to the states. Those people are so bourgeoisie and whack. It's very hard to get away with killing out there, father. Can you send someone else?" Zaby begged.

"I can't, baby. You're well trained for this type of combat, sweetie. You'll be ok."

"Ok I guess. I'm going home. I'll come see you when I'm ready to go" Zaby said leaving her father's office as he nodded his head.

Zaby was a twenty-two-year-old trained yet deadly assassin for her father. She was beautiful and looked identical to the singer, Ariana Grande. She had a tan complexion, stood five-four in height, long dark and brown hair, hazel greenish eyes, dimples, perfect jaw structure, thin eyebrows, small B-cup breast, nice toned legs with thick thighs and curves to match her perfect ample round ass.

She drove the Arabian men crazy, but she had a thing for black American men, but that was always her own secret desires.

Zaby had her own home, cars, and life outside of killing. She had her own successful clothing line and shoes. Her sister, Ummu was following her father's shoes unlike her. She wanted to make her own legacy in life.

Romell Tukes

Chapter Six

Ibague`, Colombia

Carmilla looked out her balcony glass doors of her 18,697 square foot mansion to see the beautiful orange and purple sunset rise early in the morning behind the mountain top.

Two years ago, Carmilla was one of the top federal agents in Washington, D.C after the mob and Web, the man she ended up marrying and falling in love with.

Once Web and Murda killed her father, Rafael, her brother Flaco took over the family, but he was also killed by Murda, leaving the family empire open.

Carmilla took over her family cartel. She controlled the Colombian Cartel even though it was never in her plan, but she loved the power. Now she knew how her father felt.

Since her husband's death, life had been lonely because no man could replace his love or dent he left in her heart.

Before he was killed, she had some important shit to tell him, but it was bad timing.

"Mommy, mommy, mommy," a little cute Spanish light skin toddler with curly hair yelled running into his mom's room.

"Yes, Webster," Carmilla asked picking him up.

"Can I sleep in your bed?"

"Sure, come on. I'm tired anyway baby and we got along day," she said lying in bed with her son.

When she got back in town with Web, she wanted to tell him so bad she had become pregnant with his son, but she was too scared. She never got the chance to tell him about his handsome son, Webster Jr., who looked like both of them.

Carmilla was still beautiful and eye candy, but she became a vicious savage over the years. She ran a worldwide drug trade and she planned to take over South American, but there was one family in her way. The Panamanian Cartel.

She fell asleep with her four-year-old son in her arms as she did every night when she was home in her beautiful brick mansion surrounded by goons.

***

Giudad Bolivar, Venezuela

Elena was lying beside her pool getting a tan on this hot sunny day in her red Chanel bikini showing her abs, perky big titties, and thickness as the guards were doing their job.

She was still the face of the Venezuelan Cartel and doing well for herself, even after all she been through in the recent years.

Losing her daughter, Teresa, to the ongoing war with Web and his son Murda, crushed her soul. Her heart was still crying in pain.

A couple of days ago, she received a call from a man name Stacks that informed her he had something important to talk about.

At first she was going to tell him to get lost until he told her he could help her get revenge for her daughter's death. After saying that, she set up a meeting with him at her house for tomorrow to see who the man was.

***

The Next Day

Elena was sitting at the head of her long dining room table in a black saint YSL dress looking like America's Next Top Model from overseas. She looked beautiful, as she waited for her guest, who had just arrived, followed her goons.

"Your guest has arrived."

"Good. Stacks correct?" she said looking the man up in down in his Armani suit, with his neat dreads, and trimmed beard. Elena had to admit, he was a sexy piece of chocolate.

"Yes, nice to meet you, Ms. Elena," Stacks said sitting at the end of the table admiring her beauty.

"Please, you can call me Elena. Glad you had a safe flight on my private jet but getting straight to business. How can I help?"

"I used to work with Web, until his son tried to kill me. Luckily, I had on a vest, but while everybody thought I was dead, I was watching Web and Murda's every move. This is how I know about you."

"I see," she replied.

"As time went on, I kidnapped Murda's son, which I still have. I've been holding him for a blood ransom. With your help and army, I'm sure we can take and kill everything he loves just as they did the both of us," Stacks said.

"What makes you think I can't kill Murda on my own without the help from a man I don't know from a can of paint?" she replied in Spanish accent.

"If that was the case, beauty, his whole bloodline would have been dead. You see, the truth is you don't know where to start. You're just out for blood waiting on the perfect time and this is it. Trust me, two heads is better than one."

"Ok, Stacks. I like your vision but what do you want from me?"

"Your army. You see, since Web died, Murda and his little brother, Gunna, got Brooklyn in their hands because there feeding all the wolves."

"I'ma do you one better. Since I want blood, I'm coming to New York with my men. I want Murda to die at my hands. I have a mansion in Westchester County and money, or weapons isn't an issue."

"Perfect, I'll see you in New York," Stacks said standing to leave smiling.

"Stacks," She called out to him, stopping him in his tracks. "One slip and your dead," She said seriously.

"Elena, there is only one thing I want to slip in," Stacks said sexually as she smiled.

"Be careful what you wish for."

"As long as it comes true," he said leaving her wet in her lace thongs.

***

South Boston

Gabby was driving her daughter to her cousin Missy's house in the suburb area of Boston, where she spent some time at growing up with her brother, Sergio.

Tookie's funeral was days ago. Gabby couldn't go near his grave, so she played the back as Tookie's friends, families and gang members mourned and grieved at the packed funeral.

When she found out he got killed, she grieved for weeks, unable to breathe, talk, walk, handle their business affairs, bills, or care for her daughter Crystal. She was thankful for a good babysitter and friends.

Days ago, she went to the graveyard he was killed at and one of the workers just started to talk to her about the man that was killed by a cute, redhead chick that somewhat looked like her.

At Tookie's funeral, Gabby saw a white chick with red hair in a nice Land Rover Sport watching the funeral with a smile. Gabby wrote her license plate down and tailed her to a building in Manhattan. Gabby was on a mission to find her husband's killer at any cause, so she was having her cousin babysit for a while until her mission was complete.

Chapter Seven

Manhattan, NY

Susanna Cavallari was escorted into her bar by her guards. She headed to her office because she had to do some paperwork for her bank.

Susanna was a thirty-six-year-old beautiful blonde with green eyes, a nice tan on her white skin, thick lips, and with a body of a black girl from down South. Her father was the chief of police in the city. She was the head of the Cavallari crime family in New York. Her uncle and brother, Mr. Cavallari and Vuttian, both died in prison ten years ago. They were both serving a life sentences in Green Haven Maximum security prison. Her uncle died from cancer, and Jodi killed himself in his cell.

Susanna had two well-known bars in the city she owned, two car auto shops, and three hair salons. She was very wealthy and fancy. She was the only one to carry the family legacy.

With no kids, no husband, and no boyfriend, she was able to focus on her business and Mafia family.

Now with Chelsea ahead of all the Mob families, it made her sick to her stomach because she had a strong disliking her.

Last week, she had her capo do some research on this Murda character and he came up with nothing. It was like saying a ghost's name in Brooklyn, which was odd to her.

She planned to give the situation some time, and she was sure Casper the ghost would show his face.

***

Bronx, NY

"I've been very calm, and patience is my train of thought, but Chelsea is very disappointed with your work ethic. She is missing $100,000 from one of her accounts and as her banker and accountant all of the fingers point at you," Richard said surround by goons in Marion's office.

"I have no clue what's going here," Marion said nervously loosening his tie.

"Oh, you don't? Maybe I can help bring your foggy ass memory back. Men help him reminisce," Richard said as four large men grabbed Marion out of his chair and dragged him to his office window as Richard opened it.

Marion was hanging out his window on the twenty-seventh-floor window of the skyscraper building by his feet.

"Ahhhh, pleaseeee. Ok, ok, ok. I will fix it. Please pull me back in," Marion yelled with tears in his eyes, as blood rushed his head. He was so far up he couldn't even see the people on the sidewalks clearly. They all looked like ants scurrying.

"You will pay double, correct?" Richard asked.

"Yes."

"Ok. Let him back in," Richard said smiling, seeing Marion, crying. He was shaking, trying to pull out a Newport rushing to smoke in a non-smoking building Marion was scared for his life. "Nice doing business with you. She will check her account at five p.m. and please, don't make me come back." Richard left with his guards as Marion's co-workers tried to see what was going on.

Richard Zapantino was Chelsea's go to guy and capo. He was from Venice, Italy but raised in Chicago.

He was thirty-seven, tall, skinny, scary looking and a natural killer. His father was a big snitch in the 1960's in Chicago. He brought down a lot of big-name Mob families, until his own brother killed him, then raised Richard.

Richard met Chelsea when she came to Chicago looking for her capo and she needed a real killer who was 100% Italian. Richard's name was like Jay-Z's name in Brooklyn, he was a household name, so she knew he was the man for her position. Now, he was under the Godmother of the Mafia.

***

Brooklyn, NY

The Barclay's Center was the hang out spot in Brooklyn. Everybody went there for events, concerts, dining, fun, and sightseeing.

"Oh, my God, Gunna this place is amazing. I can't believe I've been in Brooklyn this long and never been here," Ariana said sitting at a dinner table, enjoying her meal with Gunna, looking beautiful in her off white dress and red bottom heels.

"You gotta get out more, ma. You be all cooped up in that flower shop and the crib. Live your life." Gunna told her, scanning the place to see dudes staring at Ariana.

"Yeah but since my dad passed, I've been numb to living. It's like you and Murda are all I know." she said honestly.

"I feel you."

"Have you seen Murda lately?"

"For a second, but I didn't get a chance to speak to him. Sometimes bro be in his shell."

"Facts," Ariana replied eating her seafood salad.

"You ready to get out of here? I gotta go see NH."

"Ok, you can just drop me off at home," Ariana said, grabbing her iPhone, tossing it in her off white purse.

"Of course, where else are you going?"

"Boy please. I got a life. I just look boring," she said laughing as they made their way through the crowded restaurant on the lower level of the huge Barclay's center.

Once outside in the parking lot Gunna led the way to his new all black Audi R8 Spyder. This was his favorite car.

"Thanks for coming out, sis. It's always cool to build with a real soldier. Aye, you gotta tell me some war stories. I know you was over there knocking shit off," Gunna said pulling out his car keys hitting the push to start button as the Audi came to life.

"You are crazy," she said laughing as she got serious. "You strapped?" she said with a serious face.

"Yeah, why what's up?"

"Where being followed. Don't turn…"

Bloc!

Bloc!
Bloc!
Bloc!
Bloc!
Bloc!

Ariana was cut off when six gunmen came from hidden areas, shooting at them.

"Duck," Ariana yelled pulling out her .45 Desert Eagle, shooting two of the gunmen in the chest as the rest took cover.

"Shit," Gunna said as Ariana was across from him, behind a truck making a hand signal.

"Nigga, this ain't the army. On three, we light they asses up," Gunna yelled as bullets waved pass his shoulders.

Ariana and Gunna both stepped out from behind cars, shooting non-stop until two more gunmen laid there dead.

The other two men ran off towards a blue van that quickly raced out of the lot.

"One is still alive," Gunna said seeing one man trying to crawl but not getting far. Gunna shot him twice in his leg.

"Ahhhh fuck come on man," the white man screamed.

"Why are you hear?"

"Chelsea and Richard, man. I'm just a worker," he yelled in pain bleeding badly.

Boc!
Boc!
Boc!
Boc!

Ariana shot him in his face before they ran to the Audi, as sirens were nearing.

Chapter Eight

Rumson, NJ

Fernando Swanepoel was the Don in New Jersey with the biggest crime family in the state, the Swanepoel Family.

He was a mad man since the age of twenty-five, the oldest Mob family the Lavaratori's crime family took him under their wing and groomed him into a boss.

Fernando was now pushing sixty-years-old and was very successful with a small army under his command. He was all about money and peace. He hated violence because it didn't make money, instead money would be lost and good men.

With Chelsea running the show, he knew it was the worst thing that could ever happen to the Mob. He thought it was never a good idea to let the females run any family because women go off emotion, which could be deadly in business.

For years, Fernando had a chain of car dealerships in Jersey, three tax businesses, a tuxedo shop, two laundry mats and cleaners, and he ran a classy golf club he owned because he loved golfing.

He was sitting in his beautiful rich $18.5 million-dollar, 14,314 square foot mansion with twelve bedrooms, seven bathrooms that sat on three acres of land. He was waiting for his beautiful thirty-year-old wife, Celine to arrive from her trip to London, so they could make sweet love while he was off the blue pill.

***

Brooklyn, NY

"Yo I'm telling you, son. I'ma kill all them muthafuckers," Gunna said aggressively as Murda and Ariana stood under the Brooklyn bridge early in the morning.

"Are you done?"

"No, I aint done nigga. What the fuck you mean, blood? I almost lost my life to an Uncle Sam again," Gunna shouted walking back and forth on the walkway.

"Look I've been waiting to speak to the both of you, but I had to look into some shit."

"You were going to tell us at our funeral?" Gunna said, looking at Murda crazy as Ariana couldn't help but laugh "Ariana, this shit is not funny."

"I know, but just listen to him," Ariana said.

"Now you taking his side?"

"Gunna, you wilding, son. You're acting like a little bitch," Murda said in his Balmain sweatsuit as Gunna stopped walking.

"Call me a bitch one more time and *word to the Blood*, I'll knock you the fuck out! That's on the gang."

"So, what you trying to do, son?" Murda said frustrated, now face-to-face with his little brother who was taller than him but Murda had more muscle mass.

"Please, y'all need to grow up," Ariana said getting between them both. "Now, Murda please tell us why you called us," she said as he calmed down.

"We're at war again."

"With who?" Ariana asked.

"The person who killed our father," he said looking at Ariana. Gunna and Murda had different fathers.

Ariana froze because she never got to build with her pops because she was kidnapped, and by the time she was able to get away, it was too late.

"A woman named, Chelsea. She is the head of the Mafia since she killed her own father, but the crazy part is she was our uncle's wife before she killed him too," Murda said shockingly.

"This bitch is crazy," Gunna stated.

"What does she want?" Ariana asked.

"Blood. Us. Web's legacy or his bloodline. At least that's what I can put together."

"How did you find out all of this shit?" Gunna asked, thinking his brother know more than he was saying.

"Recently, I met with the man who met with Web before he was killed."

"You believe him? How do we know he didn't have anything to do with Web's death?" Ariana asked as Gunna was thinking the same thing.

"There's two reasons I do believe him. One is because his eyes said it all and I did my research on him before I went to Abu Dhabi. Two: he's sneaky."

"Okay so, what now? Obviously, they know who we are," Gunna stated.

"It's time for war," Murda said as Ariana smiled. "But Ariana, I want you to play the background until needed. We got enough men for a war."

"What? I'm well trained, Murda and I'm a big girl. She killed my father too," Ariana said getting upset.

"I know this, but I can't lose a sister, period," Murda said seriously.

"Oh, wow. This is fucked up," she said walking off towards her Benz.

"I have a new plug, Gunna and this is on another level. Are you sure you can handle work in a time of war?"

"Of course, as long as it's fire," Gunna said, relieved his brother got a new plug because he needed one after having NH kill Niño.

"Ok but don't do this plug as you did Niño."

"How did you hear about that?"

"It doesn't matter, but the price is low. Ten bands a ticket."

"No fucking way bro. That shit must be some trash."

"Trust me, Gunna. When have I ever steered you wrong?"

"Aight, but this war going to draw a lot of blood."

"I know, but one more thing. Our plug is sending us some help and I need you to look out..."

"Nigga, I'm no fucking babysitter," Gunna cut him off.

"Bro, please for me."

"You be on some other shit sometimes, bro. All we need is Ariana. You know she's like that. She got a shoot to kill shot, son.

You wilding. We need her," Gunna said looking at Ariana in her Benz, pissed off.

"I can't, Gunna. She's my sister. I can't let nothing happen to her. I wouldn't be able to live with myself. We risk our lives in these streets, so our family wouldn't have to and she family."

"I understand that, but at least let her go on some easy shit here and there. Don't leave her out, bro. She a killer just like us. You let her put in work sometimes and I'll babysit whoever," Gunna said smiling, leaving him no choice.

"Shit, Gunna. Why you always gotta make shit hard? Ok, but you going with her on them missions," Murda said as Gunna waved her to come here.

"Good. We have a deal. When is this help coming?"

"This week."

"Ok, good. Let me know the place and time and I'm on it, Blood," Gunna said as Ariana approached them with her arms crossed.

"What do you want?" she said rudely looking in her brother's green eyes with her bright hazel eyes.

"You can put in some work but he's going to be with you," Murda said pointing at Gunna.

"Yess! Thank you, brother," she said hugging him tightly.

"Just be aware that this shit is going to get nasty," Murda said walking off to his Wraith parked next to Ariana's Benz truck.

Chapter Nine

Rye, NY

Stacks was invited to Elena's home in Westchester, a rich gated neighborhood near the Playland amusement park. Her guards picked him up in a Tahoe SUV from Mount Vernon. He had no clue she was even in town, but it was perfect because now the party could get started.

She told him to wear swimming trunks as he did under his Nike tracksuit. With her army and his plans, Stacks could feel himself back on top soon, very soon.

When the driver and guards pulled into the driveway, Stacks saw the gracious front porch to the airy two-story entrance foyer with the spectacular view of the eighteenth-century mansion.

The palace was 16,179 square feet, with forty-five-foot ceilings, heated floors, two levels, walk-in closets, seven bedrooms, five bathrooms, six car garage, two pools, one large and one medium, a basement bar and family room.

Elena had this mansion for years. It was really for her daughter because she used to love coming to New York to shop and have fun.

"The boss waits for you in the back area.," a big Spanish man stated, as he posted in the lobby with a gang of security guards hanging out.

"Thanks," Stacks said making his way out to the back.

The sun was beaming today as he looked around for Elena. Using his hand as a sun blocker, he finally saw Elena under the water swimming laps at a fast pace.

She stopped when she saw him and climbed out the pool.

"Stacks," Elena said in a red Gucci bikini holding her nice big round titties in place, as her abs were chiseled, her toned legs, thick curves, long wet hair was dripping. He was at a loss for words.

She looked like a Baywatch lifeguard. His dick was hard as she approached, feeling embarrassed.

"Elena," he replied amazed at how beautiful she was without make up.

"Someone is happy to see me and it's not your face. Let's go for a swim. Take your clothes off," Elena said walking back into the pool as he watched her phat ass clap left to right.

Stacks stripped down to his Balmain swimming trunks and followed her into the pool. When she saw his big chest, big arms, and eight pack, her pussy was wetter than the water. Stacks still worked out daily to maintain his appearance.

"Nice body, but I assume you have plans set up. My crew is flying out here this week, but I want you to take your time. I want this to go perfect." Elena said leaning on the edge of the pool.

"It will. I'm putting the finishing touches on my plans. I'm just locating any potential threats."

"Perfect. I got faith in you," she said as she saw him staring at her tits. "It's rude to stare and not say anything," she flirted.

"I have a lot to say in so many ways."

"I'm a person of action," she said smiling, as he made his way in front of her before kissing her soft lips. She wrapped her arms around his neck as he slipped his trunks off and fingered her tight pussy. "Uhmmm," she moaned.

Stacks moved her panties to the side and lifted her as he slowly penetrated her with his big dick getting her fired up. She moved her hips back and forth.

"Ugh! Fuck me," she moaned, leaning her head back as he fucked the shit out of her. Stacks never felt a pussy so tight besides Jamika's, as Elena pussy lips wrapped tightly around his dick. He drover deeper and deeper until she climaxed, almost crying as his cum poured into the pool.

"Shit," Stacks gritted as he released inside of her.

"Oh, my god, papi. You're a machine," she said turning over arching her ass up as he got behind her and her wide phat ass as he began fucking her doggy-style. "Ohhh yesss, si, si, si. Ohh!

Mmm," she groaned as he picked up the pace. She pushed her ass back into him, making a clapping sound.

Their moans grew louder until she finally let out a scream, climaxing seconds later. Stacks followed close behind, shooting his load of thick cum on her back.

Once they got themselves together, they talked business and Elena had her maid prepare a Spanish meal for Stacks. They then went to her master bedroom and fucked until dawn.

***

Bogota, Colombia

Today, Carmilla was meeting with the Panamanian Cartel capo, which, from Carmilla's understanding, was the boss' son, but she wanted to know why Patricia Henriquez couldn't meet with her.

Carmilla arrived at a small coffee shop in the capital of Colombia to see a young man with a baby face in a suit with two guards behind him watching her and her eight men crew every move.

"Ah, Mrs. Carmilla. How do you do?" The young man said as Carmilla sat down.

"Who the fuck are you and why did you call me? I only speak to the head of the families," she said pissed off, looking into his young blue eyes.

"Yes. I'm Juan Henriquez. My mother isn't feeling well, so she asked me to come cut and speak to you. Your drug trade is becoming an issue for us. We sell weight to the same families as you do and your prices are cutting our throats. You basically stole our clients. When Rafael and Flaco were in charge, they respected the boards and we only ask you do the same please," Juan said in Spanish

"The country is big enough," Carmilla responded in Spanish. "But not for the two of us, brother. Her guards shot both of his men behind him, killing them. Juan had the look of fear in his face as Carmilla pulled out a handgun, before shooting him thirteen times in the face. She left out the empty coffee shop as two waiters hid behind the cash register shaken.

***

New York City

Gunna just walked into the airport in a red Versace outfit with Versace loafers to match as his WS Cuban link chains that hung from his neck. Gunna had no clue who he was looking for. All he knew was an Arabian man named Zaby, so he placed a sign on his Audi door that said Zaby. He didn't have patience, so he wanted to look for this nigga himself.

He hated babysitting especially a grown man, but he gave his brother his word and he was going to stick to it.

Gunna saw all types of beautiful women but one caught his eye. She had a bronze tan complexion with a nice body in her jeans, designer shades, long hair in a ponytail, she looked like a better and thicker Ariana Grande to him.

"Damn that bitch bad," he mumbled as he got closer to the woman waiting in the baggage claim line.

"Excuse me, ma, but I believe I lost something in your purse," Gunna said skipping the line, as the woman took off her shades, confused as Gunna was stuck in her beautiful eyes.

"You must have the wrong person," the woman said in clear English

"No, I don't because when I saw you seconds ago, you stole my heart," Gunna said showing his handsome smile as the woman blushed then frowned.

"You're so corny. Excuse me," she said, grabbing her Fendi suitcase, racing away from the stranger in her Gucci heels matching her Gucci jeans, blouse, and shades.

"Fuck it."

"You were close, bud. She's outta our class," a young white man said, grabbing his bag walking off

"Hater," Gunna mumbled looking for Zaby so he could leave. After ten minutes of no signs of an Arabian man, he walked outside to his Audi to see a ticket on his windshield for blocking the business entrance and fire zone.

"Fucking bitch," Gunna shouted, kicking his Audi tire because he hated tickets. He heard someone giggle, which got him fired up until he saw it was the pretty woman, he just tried to holler at standing there laughing.

"That's why you're going be laughing in an Uber," Gunna said mad.

"Well it looks like you're my Uber. I'm Zaby," she said seeing her name on his car door as he was speechless. "Out of words now?" she said smiling.

"Zayid sent you?" he asked to be sure because Murda never said if it was a male or female.

"Yes, that's my father."

"Uhmmm. Whatever, get in," he said not even helping her. She shook her head and put her suitcase in his trunk, but she knew he was embarrassed from what took place as they rode in silence.

Romell Tukes

Chapter Ten

Atlanta, GA

Katherine was a beautiful Dominican woman from Washington Heights, NY and Web's first love. She was the mother of their daughter, Ariana. When her daughter told her about Web's murder, she was sick.

Web was a great man. The greatest she ever met in her lifetime. That's why every time she thought about what she did to him, it made her feel bad because he didn't deserve it.

Even though she only stole a couple of million from him, the principle of it made her feel like shit to this day.

Katherine ran three hair salons. Two in the urban areas of Atlanta and one in Buckhead, the rich white people section.

It was ninety-nine degrees in the city today and Katherine had a handful of new clients and old clients with appointments.

She hopped out her gray Infiniti Q60 in tight jeans, showing her thick curves and nicely shaped plump ass.

As soon as she walked into her salon, her five workers were over filled with clients as it was every Saturday morning in Hair Central Salon.

Katherine grabbed couple of clients and got to work, starting her long day.

***

Hours Later

It was ten at night and she was drained on her way home. Katherine hated when the weekend came, but her salons were the biggest in Atlanta, so everybody came by. She was on her way home as she was texting while driving a new young man, she met days ago at the park on her morning run.

His name was Randell, and he was from Texas. He was in Atlanta doing movie films. He was tall, muscular, sexy, well-mannered and just Katherine's type.

The two set up a date for tomorrow, but she had more than a date planned. She needed some good dick. Her pussy hadn't been touched in years because she was so busy with her career.

She was finally home. Something told her to text Ariana to see how she was doing. Since her daughter moved to New York, they been distant even though Katherine took time out to go visit her a couple of times.

When she met Murda, she saw so much of him in Web it was scary. Not to mention how handsome he was. She knew his mother because Web never kept his affairs a secret.

Ariana's decision of staying in New York to run a flower shop didn't sit well with Katherine, but her daughter seemed happy, so she rode with it.

Once inside her mini mansion, she turned on the lights, only to be tackled by two large men as they pinned her to the floor roughly as she tried to squirm out of their hold but was unlucky.

"Katherine, relax love. It's ok," a woman's voice said coming out the kitchen eating an apple, with two big men behind her.

Katherine remembered the women coming into her salon earlier because she was the one who did her red hair.

"You bitch! I should have fucked your hair up," Katherine said stretched out on the floor making Chelsea laugh.

"This isn't personal. You just loved the wrong man. There will be many more coming with you," Chelsea said, grabbing a 44 Bulldog handgun from one of her security guards and shooting Katherine four times in her heart. She watched as she choked on her own blood and smiled as if it was a scene from a love movie.

"Let's go gentlemen. I want to hit up a club out here. My pussy is itching," Chelsea said walking out the house in a white and red Chanel bodycon suit with nothing under to seduce men in her six-inch heels.

***

Brooklyn, NY

Murda and his man Ja entered Brooklyn in his Rolls Royce Wraith Black Badge edition all black with the stars in the ceiling.

"So, when this shit supposed to be popping off?" Ja asked, slumped in the passenger seat as Murda whipped the Wraith through a nice sunny day on these Brooklyn streets, heading to his condo.

"Soon. I need everybody to be on point and have your teams intact." Murda said pulling into a car wash in Bed-Stuy.

"Yo son, we got you. Everybody's waiting on your move, big homie."

"Aight," Murda stated hopping out as he was fourth in line, but he wanted to buy some smell goods for his car from the small booth outside.

Tat!
Tat!
Tat!
Tat!
Tat!
Tat!
Tat!
Tat!
Tat!
BOOM!
BOOM!
BOOM!
BOOM!
BOOM!
BOOM!
BOOM!

Shooters surrounded the car wash, gunning for Murda dressed in all black except one person who made their face known, Stacks.

Ja took out three shooters as he ran to cover for Murda, who was going bullet for bullet with Stacks, but his Glock 17 was no match for the assault rifle SK.

Tat!
Tat!
Tat!
Tat!
Tat!

The windows to the carwash booth shattered as employees ran the ones that wasn't already dead.

Boc!
Boc!
Boc!
Boc!
Boc!
Boc!
Boc!
Boc!

Murda took out two of Stacks shooters as he hide behind the tail of one of the SUV he came in.

"It's six of them left, Ja. We gotta get out of here I got nine shots left" Murda said ducked off behind the booth as bullets kept coming down on them like rain.

"I'ma cover you on five," Ja said as both men ran towards the Wraith, shooting at the two trucks killing three more of Stacks gunmen. They climbed in the Wraith reversing out the lot as bullets hit the bulletproof front window doing nothing as Stacks saw them get away.

"What the fuck was that?" Ja shouted once the Wraith was far away from the mayhem.

"It's time for war! You know what's up," Murda said as blood rushed through his head to see the man who had kidnap his son years ago.

"Who was that black dude with the beard and dreads?" Ja said as NYPD police raced past them.

"Stacks."

"Hold on, Stacks from the Pink Houses? I heard somebody killed him years ago," Ja asked as his heart was still racing from the adrenaline rush.

" I thought I did but he survived and kidnapped my son and now he's back, so I still think my son is alive, so that's my mission, but we still gotta worry about the Mob, so put everything in place."

"Copy, big homie. Sorry to hear about your seed. I had no clue," Ja stated.

"I know. It's all God's plan," Murda said dazed off thinking about what just happened.

Romell Tukes

Chapter Eleven

Long Island, NY

Gabby was driving her new Dodge SRT Challenger Hellcat Redeye with a black hood and tints. She was driving through North Hampton to visit her cousin, Phoebe Glipino who was a Mob wife to Orlando Glipino. Orlando was serving a double life sentence in the feds for killing two police officers and running the Glipino Crime family.

She drove through a gated rich community with big manicured yards and the biggest mansions she ever saw.

For the past few days, she been doing her research on the red head lady she saw at Tookie's funeral and downtown.

She knew the woman's name was Chelsea and she was the daughter of a man named Donvito, but that was all she knew, which was way she was here today.

House 1719 was at the beginning of the block. Gabby passed twice, the mansion was big and yellow with glass double doors and a Porsche Macon GTS and a Corvette ZR1 both parked in the driveway.

Gabby parked and made her way to the doorstep. The porch light was bright as she knocked twice.

Phoebe came to the door in a robe smiling ear to ear when she saw Gabby because she hadn't saw her little cousin in years.

"Oh, Gabby, look at you sweetie. Come," Phoebe said walking into her antique wide pine floored home.

They went and sat down in the living room where Phoebe had kettle of hot tea ready and two teacups.

"Thanks for meeting me."

"My pleasure. You look so good. Just like your mother. I'm sorry to hear about your brother, darling. You know how this life this."

"I do. How's Orlando?" Gabby asked as Phoebe poured them both some mint tea.

"He's well getting old. He's praying for an appeal to go through. He's in Florida somewhere at some prison, but you just missed Lily she stopped by. You know she is dating a black NFL football player. You know my father is turning in his grave."

Phoebe came from a rich Mafia family. She helped raise Gabby. She owned yachts, five mansions, vacation homes and every type of luxury car out with Germany engines. She was fifty-seven years old, but thanks to plastic surgery, she was able to avoid wrinkles, saggy breast and skin.

"I have a couple of questions because I know your still connected with the Mob ties,"

"Of course, love. Who do you need whacked?" Phoebe stated seriously drinking her tea in sips.

"I need to know about Chelsea," Gabby said as Phoebe spit her tea out on to her floor.

"Excuse me, wow. Are you sure it's her, Gabby because if so, we're not talking about regular Mobsters? That bitch is the devil."

"Tell me everything you can."

"For starters, whatever happens, keep me and my family name away from her."

"I promise."

"She poisoned her father just to receive the royal family crown. Now she is the Godmother over all families. Word is she killed a very powerful man named Web and now she is about to start a war in New York. Gabby, this woman is very dangerous. Whatever you have going on with her, please run the other way." Phoebe said seriously scared for her cousin.

"What other families are under her? "Gabby asked.

"The Swanepoel Family in Jersey, the Janard Family in Brooklyn and of course my good friends the Cavaliari Family," Phoebe said because she was good friends with Susanna's family, especially her father. He was a ranking officer in the city.

"Ok thank you, I gotta go. I love you."

"Gabby, please be safe," Phoebe said letting her out wondering what Gabby got herself into.

***

Weeks later
Brooklyn, NY

Ariana had just got back from her mom's funeral in Atlanta and she was very depressed and hurt due to the death of her mom.

Ariana's neighbor told her she saw a red head lady leaving Katherine's home with four big white men in suits.

Without thinking too hard on it, she already knew who it was. This was why she was waiting at this low-key diner in downtown BK to meet with Murda.

When she saw the black and blue Bugatti Chiron Sport pull into the parking lot with two Land Rover Ranger Rover SVR behind him, she knew it was Murda and he was war ready.

Murda walked into the diner, dripped out in Givenchy designer with a vest under.

"So what's popping?" Murda said realizing there was something wrong with her.

"She killed my mother," Ariana said trying to hold back her real emotions as he hugged her.

"Fuck, I'm sorry. We're going to get her, sis. Trust me. So much is going on so fast, I'm overwhelmed. The nigga who kidnapped my son tried to kill me a couple weeks ago."

"Wow."

"Yeah and I'm not even going to tell Jamika just yet. She been doing well with work and all," Murda said.

"I think you should tell her soon because your son can still be out there." Ariana said in her soft voice thinking about her mom.

"I'ma figure it out but I'ma hunt this bitch down, sis. Don't worry about nothing," Murda said as they talked for a couple of hours before going different ways with Chelsea on both of their minds.

Romell Tukes

Chapter Twelve

Downtown Brooklyn

Silvio Janeiro was leaving his law firm office. This was one of three he had in Brooklyn. He was a civil lawyer, but his employees were criminal lawyers mostly.

Silvio was a very connected man. He was connected to the Mayor, Governor, and DEA. He was a big name in the politics. Unaware to most, he lived a double life. Besides being a wealthy lawyer, he was also the boss of the Janerio Crime Family in Brooklyn.

At thirty-five years old, he had everything one can ask for. He had money, power, success, women, and happiness. He was tall, handsome, muscular built, short dark hair, blue eyes, and a nice smile.

He was pushing his twin turbo V6 $2.1 million-dollar Ashton Martin Valhalla through the city streets on his way to a meeting with a client this morning.

Silvio grew up in Williamsburg, BK, a middle-class section filled with Jewish families and Mobsters.

His parents came from Rome, Italy as immigrants and worked hard to take care of Silvio, including putting him in college at an Ivy League school in California.

He became a self-made Mob boss through his cousin Rio who was killed by Joe Da Don years ago, leaving him to keep the Janeiro Crime Family name alive.

Silvio had a crew of killers within the family ready for this war but didn't need to draw attention to himself because he could jeopardize everything, he worked so hard for in life.

***

Brooklyn
King Plaza Mall

Gunna was in the mall with Zaby as she was shopping, being sure to hit every designer store in the building. He already made two trips to his Bentley dropping her bags off.

Zaby was staying at one of his condos on Court St. The two been spending a lot of time with each other getting to know one either.

Gunna thought she was going to be a stuck-up bitch living off her daddy's money, but she was a down -to -earth chick and she had her own bag. He respected that.

The only thing he didn't see in her was her being an assassin or killer because she was too girly. She wore a facial mask before she went to bed.

"Zaby, I gotta go do something in an hour," Gunna said following her around in a Christian Louboutin store looking at shoes in glass boxes.

"Gunna, can you please wait outside? You don't have to follow me in a store," she said giving him a cute look.

"Man, whatever yo. Just hurry up, my nigga," Gunna said storming out talking to himself as she laughed. She loved to get him mad it was so easy and funny.

After finding two nice fly ass pairs of Christian Louboutin's, she paid $12,816 on her black card and left. She been shopping all morning. She loved shopping in New York because they had every designer outlet one can imagine.

"Happy? I'm done. Here," she said handing him her bag as she walked out the store in a Miu Miu two piece with heels, as her hair sat in a bun. She looked sexy.

"More shoes?" Gunna said feeling the two boxes in the bag.

"No, they're for you."

"Me? You don't even know my shoe size."

"You're a size forty-eight in designer shoes," she said as his eyebrows raised because she was right, and nobody ever brought him shit expect Murda.

"Thank you but you didn't have too."

"Oh, my God shut up," she added, walking upstairs as a gang of dudes was looking at her sexually. She shook her head. She was used to the attention, especially in her county.

"Y'all niggas see something y'all like?" Gunna said clutching his pistol on his hips as the four thugs quickly shook their heads hell no

"It's cool, Gunna. Come on. Let's get out of here," she said grabbing his arm as everybody was looking.

"Bitch ass niggas," Gunna yelled as they walked into the lot filled with cars.

"It's ok, cutie," Zaby said playing with him as he shot her an evil look. "Ok, gangsta," she added as something told her to look to her left. "It's a hit," Zaby yelled, pushing Gunna on the floor as bullets weaved passed his head. Zaby pulled out her 9mm with a thirty-round clip from her lower back and shot three shooters clean in the head.

Gunna saw four shooters coming the other direction as he got up from the floor busting.

Boc!

Boc!

Boc!

Boc!

Boc!

Boc!

Boc!

"There's more," Zaby said seeing seven more Spanish men shooting SK9's and Ak-47's

Zaby and Gunna were back peddling, taking out the whole crew as they were getting close to his Bentley.

Zaby got on one knee, hitting four gunmen as the last two took cover because she hadn't missed a shot yet.

She was so busy shooting she didn't see Elena come out her hiding spot.

"Zaby," Gunna yelled blocking Zaby from the bullets. He got shot twice in his shoulder as he fired back busting out the windows to a pickup truck almost taking the pretty bitches head off.

Ten mall cops came running out with guns firing as Gunna and Zaby made it to the Bentley. The the Spanish men and Elena ran off.

Once far away from the shootout, Gunna was in serious pain.

"I think I need to get to a hospital," Gunna moaned in pain holding his shoulder as Zaby raced the Bentley to the condo because she was well trained for this type of emergency.

"Nigga stop crying."

"What the fuck you mean? I got blood all over my seats and I'm dying," he said as she was laughing so hard.

***

Hours later

Gunna was laying on his living room black leather couch in pain as Zaby was cleaning and sewing his two wounds.

"Gunna, the bullets went in and out. You will be ok. I'm done" Zaby said taking the bloody rags, thread and nails, and alcohol to the trash.

Gunna sat up shirtless showing his well-defined body as she couldn't help but stare once she walked back into the living sitting next to him.

"Thanks for saving me back there," she said looking at him.

"You saved me. It's the least I can do."

"I really like you Gunna."

"I like you too," he added looking into her bright eyes he always got lost in. Zaby moved in closer, kissing him while he frenched kiss her back. Within minutes of foreplay, they were both in the bedroom ass naked.

Gunna eyed her toned body, nice little titties and the prettiest tan pussy he ever saw. It shaved bald, a small swollen clit, thin straight pussy lip with a phat outside plump.

She opened her legs wider as Gunna entered her tight, wet little pussy as she slid back moaning, digger her nails into his back as he drove deeper into her.

"Uhmmmm. yessss ohhhh," she screamed.

His thick cock was now pumping in and out of her harder. With every thrust, she loosened up.

"Fuck me harder more. Uggghh," she yelled.

Gunna was hitting her G-spot as his dick and balls continued to slap loudly against her wetness while her moans turned into screams and cries then orgasms.

"Oh, my God I never felt nothing like this," she said as he turned her on her side and cocked her left leg in the air. He fucked the dear life out of her, almost tossing her off the bed from his long strokes.

After they both climaxed, Gunna placed her at the edge of the bed and pushed her legs behind her head staring at the small open hole in the middle as clear cum was pouring out she was so wet.

Gunna fucked her at a slowly pace as she helped hold her legs.

"Uhhhh shittt.she scream with her mouth stuck open as her pussy gripped his dick as he went faster. "I'm cummmmmin-nnggggg," she cried. climaxing on his dick. He continued to pound her pussy out as she took it like a champ until he came inside of her pussy filled with creamy semen.

"I want to taste. Can I?" she asked sexually.

"I want to taste you too," he said as they got in a sixty-nine position and sucked each other off like it was a porno.

Romell Tukes

Chapter Thirteen

Brooklyn, NY
Pink Houses Projects

Ms. Sanders was a sixty-year-old black woman who was the best babysitter in the projects for over thirty years.

She used to have a daycare years ago until she retired and just wanted to live a regular old lady lifestyle.

Ms. Sanders raised a lot of legends that came from the Pink Houses and one of those men was Stacks. He was her favorite and she would do anything for him.

When Stacks brought the newborn baby boy to her to look after him, she asked no questions. He was paying her fifteen thousand dollars every sixty days to look after him, which was a plus.

For sixty she still had it. She was brown skin, gray hair, thick, saggy breast, and beautiful. Her thirty-two-year-old boyfriend just left. They were fucking all night. He would put the old butt on bedrest for days when he came around.

She was making a baby bottle for the toddlerwho would awake from his nap any minute. She had no clue the baby was kidnapped and belonged to a kid she used to babysit.

***

Manhattan, NY

Gunna and NH were both riding in his white Benz G550 truck with tints to the address Murda gave him earlier when they got together.

Zayid finally shipped the work to a cargo dock in Manhattan. By the time they got there, everything would be waiting in a black van for them parked across the street in a Barnes & Noble parking lot.

Murda made it clear to Gunna, that only him and NH are to pick up the shipments then after that, it was on them. That way they can avoid police, rats, and the stick-up boys.

"I can't believe you got shot bro. I know that shit hurt like a muthafucker," NH said as Gunna was zoned out.

"Huh?"

"Damn, brody. You've been on some weird shit only day," NH added shaking his head as they drove across a bridge, into morning traffic.

"May bad son shit been brazy. You know we at war, Loc, so niggas be coming from all over to get at us. Murda laying low, putting plans into motion and now we got a new plug because that shit from Niño was gone weeks ago. I had some more shit in the stash, but you done with that. It's just so much shit popping off at once it's hard to stay focused, you heard."

"I feel you cuz it's a drought in Brooklyn right now. I'ma flood the streets and handle the streets," NH said.

"Facts."

"Oh yeah, mama Love asked about you the other day when I went to see her out her on the lower eastside. She moved from Brooklyn." NH said referring to his mother who was a NYPD officer.

"Tell her hi, I know she be worried about us."

"Hell yeah, that's why I stay away from her cuz she be driving me crazy, but what's up with that foreign chick you brought to the hood? Bro everybody was talking about shawty even the bitches," NH said.

"That's Zaby. She's wifey now bro. She's a real killer, bro. Shawty some trained assassin from the Middle East," Gunna said smiling thinking about Zaby and their new relationship.

"Damn that's crazy. How the fuck that happen? She got friends?" NH replied laughing as they pulled into Barnes & Noble's parking lot to see customers going in and out the bookstore early this morning.

"There it go," NH said pointing at the van parked alone next to a light pole.

"Ok you tail me back to the spot. Drive the speed limit. This ain't the time to get pulled over or we going to have to put on a movie."

"Nigga that's why they call me Spike Lee."

"You and Spike Lee ain't got shit in common. He turned into an Uncle Tom and you ducking Uncle Tom," Gunna said as NH hopped out.

***

Brooklyn

An hour later, Gunna pulled into the back off the rundown house with NH behind him. The building was a two-story home that was under construction.

Gunna brought six homes like this around Brooklyn to fix them up and sell them to homeowners or rent them out to the poor.

"You think we should call the homies?" Gunna stated hopping out the Benz truck as NH climbed out the van, smoking a blunt of Kush.

"That's on you, but I can drop them niggas shit off to them," NH said shrugging his shoulders not caring.

"You will have to drop work off to Bed-Stuy, Brownsville, East New York, Red Hook, Fort Green, Thompkins, Marcy, and your hood, bro. You will drive yourself crazy. Let's see what we are dealing with anyway." Gunna said.

"Facts because I couldn't even see what was back there with the wall behind me," NH said as Gunna opened the double back doors. Both men froze numb thinking it was unreal.

There were tons of keys stacked from the floor to the roof, wall to wall, and almost about to fall out the back door. It was so packed with work.

Both men never saw this much work added together in their lifetime.

"I was riding around with that?" NH said unable to see any room in the back.

"We're going to need some help," Gunna said wondering who the fuck would ship this much work to a person. Murda told him Zayid was big time and now he believed him, but he made a mental note to ask Zaby what the fuck he got himself into.

Gunna knew it was over 5,000 keys in the back. It would take him weeks to move this type of work, but he could feel his hand itching.

***

Turbo, Colombia
Weeks later

Carmilla was at her beach house talking to an old friend on the phone that knew nothing of her new life. Her friend was an FBI agent. She was close with before she retired.

She was always keeping Carmilla posted on the big cases and juicy gossip within the FBI in NYC and D.C.

Carmilla just hung up her office phone looking out her windows at the beach thinking about what her friend just told her. Apparently, there was a man she believed to be moving more keys then Steve Wonder ever touched in his life.

The name Gunna was brought up to her, but her friend informed her the FBI wasn't on to him yet because he was to smart, but she had been hearing his name.

Carmilla never heard of the name, but she needed a client in New York to help move her work, so if her friend was right about this Gunna person, then she would be paying him a visit soon.

Going to New York or even hearing about it, brought too many emotions to her heart, especially the thought of Web.

Chapter Fourteen

Lower Westside, NY

Silvio was doing some extra work tonight because he received ten new caseloads earlier. All his employees were gone. It was close to ten at night and Chelsea had just texted him and asked him if she could stop by. He left the front door open and informed his guards downstairs in the lobby to let her up.

"Silvio," Chelsea called out walking into his very large polished classy office with a view of the city and Hudson River.

" In the back," he yelled as she walked into his office, wearing a Miu Miu devil red dress with a slit down the middle, exposing her breast and stomach but barely covering her nipples as her back was out.

When Silvio saw her, he got extremely horny as any man would.

"Hey, I just came to check on you and see how things were going because I know how busy you are with your law firms."

"Oh yeah of course, but I'm well. My army is at our command when needed. Work is work," he said leaning back in his chair as she walked around his office.

"I don't normally mix business with pleasure but a one-night quickie won't hurt nobody, especially if it's our little secret. What do you think of that, Silvio?" Chelsea said walking over to him moving his chair in front of her

"I agree," he said as she slid between his legs and unbuckled his slacks pulling out his eight-and-a-half-inch hard-on penis as she placed her lips around his tip.

She slowly bopped her head up and down on his swollen dick as he moaned, while her wide mouth engulfed his nice size dick with her red hair was all over his lap.

Chelsea deep throated his cock down her windpipe. "Uhmmmm," she moaned going faster as she sucked and made a slurping noise, leaving his chair dripping wet with pre-cum and salvia.

"Damn it. I'm about to nut," he said, squeezing his muscles as she continued to suck on the tip while fondling with his balls until he came in her mouth. She spit it back out on his dick and stood up.

She bent over and lifted her dress up as he saw her big ass with her nice pink hairless pussy.

"Fuck me hard. I've been a bad girl," she said as he placed his big hands on her hips and slid his erection into her warm pussy that felt tight. He started off slow then she started to throw her ass on him almost knocking his dick out of her love box.

Silvio was losing control. Her ass was too much for him to handle so he pinned her ass down and fucked her hard and rough.

"Yesss mmmmm, fuck me good," she yelled holding on his desk as her titties flew everywhere.

He thrusted his hips into her back with force, every time as her pussy compressed his dick in a circular motion as she came on his cock.

"Thank you," she said as cum was running down her legs as she fixed her dressed as Silvio got dressed also.

"For what?"

"For the nut. I'll see you soon," she said leaving as if nothing happened

"Damn that crazy bitch got some good pussy," Silvio said honestly walking to his bathroom to clean himself off.

***

Queens, NY

Richard was out at a sport bar talking to a cute snow bunny he met an hour ago. The place was packed with people watching the Jets vs Eagles game.

Richard loved sports, so he would come here every Sunday alone to drink, eat, watch the games, and bag beautiful like Emmy, the sexy blonde in a Dior white mini dress and heels. She caught everybody's eye in the room, but Richard was on her since he saw her.

The two been drinking, laughing, talking about everything from sports, TV, music, and her job as a hair stylist and painter.

"How about we finish that at my place?" Richard finally stated looking at her breast and lips knowing she was going to be a lion in the bed.

"I don't know about that. How about we go to my place," she said smiling as he agreed quickly and they both left, feeling tipsy from all the liquor they consumed.

"You want to take your car or mine?" Richard asked looking at her perfect nice ass in her dress.

"I came in an Uber. I don't drink and drive," she said.

"Well I do" he said getting inside of his black Maserati Granturismo Coupe SP with tints.

She led him through the dark New York city streets until he made it to a building on the lower eastside.

"This is it. I just moved here, so its a little empty," she said as he parked in an empty parking spot.

"As long as you got a bed."

"I do and then some. I'm a little freaky," she said as they entered her brick apartment complex.

Inside the apartment, the place was empty with a couch and a couple of boxes on the wood floors.

"You just moved in here today?"

"Something like that," she said walking into the bedroom that looked like a torture chamber with whips, cuffs, hanging bars, a steel dildo, silver balls, a bed with chains, and choker collars everywhere.

"Wow freaky ain't the word," Richard said never seeing no shit like this.

"How about we start it off with me sucking this dick," Emmy said grabbing a handful of nuts because his dick was tiny, yet hard as a rock.

"I'm with that. You going to chain me up?" he said laughing.

"Yeah, get naked," she said as he followed orders turned on by the scene. Once naked, he laid on the bed as Emmy cuffed him to the chains welded on the four corners.

"Ok I'll be right back," she said smiling.

"He gets soft quick, so hurry up."

Emmy went into her bathroom swaying her hips. Seconds later, she came back with a tray full of sharp utensils.

"What's that for?" he asked wondering what type of freaky shit she was planning.

"I plan to utilize them love. I'm a firm believer in karma," she said as his eyes widened, and heart raced as he saw her malignancy look.

"Look Emmy I'm not into this. We can get a raincheck."

"Call me Gabby, please," she said putting on rubber gloves and picking up two sharp objects. "Now tell me everything you know about Chelsea since you work for her," Gabby said as she traced a blade up his legs towards his dick.

"Look please I don't know -ahhhhh!" he yelled as she stuck the blade in his thigh, cutting it open. She then placed rubber balls in his mouth. She stabbed his other thigh as he gritted in pain crying.

"You ready to talk? Just nod twice." she said as she then stabbed him in his balls. He nodded his head ready to talk, praying she didn't do it again.

Richard told Gabby everything before she slit his throat six times and cut his body into pieces. She bagged it up into a black garbage bag. Gabby cleaned up her new home and went to get rid of Richard's car. She made a stop to drop his body off at Chelsea's condo across town.

Chapter Fifteen

Soho, NY

Murda waited inside of a tea shop for Tookie's wife who reached out to him. He hadn't saw her since the funeral for her husband. He wondered what Gabby wanted because he was a busy man and time wasn't on his side.

He had Ja and a crew waiting outside in the parking lot just in case Chelsea tried some dumb shit.

Murda saw Gabby walking inside looking like an average cute white girl in jeans, a blouse, heels, a purse and her long blonde hair in a ponytail. Tookie told him how deadly Gabby was, but he just didn't see it in her because she looked like a ditzy white girl.

"Gabby how are you doing?" Murda said standing to hug her then pulling out her seat for her before she sat like a true gentleman.

"Thank you, but I'm well, Murda. Just staying focused."

"How's the baby?"

"Great!"

"Would you like to order some tea?"

"No thank you. This will be fast, but thanks for coming out. Anyway, I found out who killed my husband. It was a lady named Chelsea."

"I fucking knew it," Murda said banging his fist on the table as a couple of noisy people looked at him scared to death.

"One of the graveyard workers described her to the tee, but I'm going handle her."

"Gabby, I'ma take care of it. Please she is way dangerous. My people are looking for her as we speak."

"Murda I understand your concern, but I can handle myself. I just came to tell you that because I thought you should know," Gabby said grabbing her purse.

"I know, but you're family and I don't want to see nothing happen to you."

"Thanks, but I should be the least of your worry. You know Chelsea's capo Richard?" she asked.

"Yeah, I've been doing my research on him, but I'm coming up short. You know him?"

Gabby pulled out a small Ziplock bag with a finger inside and tossed it on the table as she stood to leave.

"Look no more," Gabby said with a fake smile as she walked out the shop.

Murda looked at the bloody finger and so did an old couple next to him trying to figure out if that was a real finger.

He placed the bag in his Dior for Men blazer coat pocket as he left thinking about Gabby and how Tookie may have been truthful when he informed him how crazy Gabby was.

***

Manhattan, NY

"Ohhhhhhmmm," Susanna moaned loudly as Brian sucked on her pink pussy lips. Her bald pussy was dripping wet as she moaned and appreciated his tongue game. "Suck it, Brian," she yelled as he teased her swollen, enlarged clit as her hips grinded to the motion of his tongue.

Brian placed two fingers in her pussy that wasn't too tight or too loose. He finger fucked her while licking her clit like a pro.

"Shitttt! Oh, my fucking, God I'm cummingg," she shouted as her head leaned back. She climaxed hard as cum squirted all over her living room carpet and leather couch. She took some deep breaths as he was still eating her out. She had to force him off her naked body.

"Get a grip on yourself," Susanna said placing a robe around her body, which was perfect with two percent body fat.

Brian went to clean off her sticky juices from his handsome face. He looked like Brad Pitt in his prime with short blonde hair, blue eyes, a five o'clock shadow, tall, skinny, tattoos, and full-blooded Italian.

He was Susanna's capo and his gun game was up to par. He was from the little Italy area of the city and was raised into the Mob by his father Freddy. Brian was only twenty-eight and owned a chain of pizza shops in every borough of the city.

Susanna and him only had oral intercourses where he would only eat her out when she was horny, but that was good enough for him. He loved the sweet taste of her pussy, even though she never helped him get his rocks off because she told him his dick was too small and weird looking.

"Boss, I got all of our men ready for war, as you asked. What now?" Brian asked walking on to the condo outside terrace where the stars were so close, you could touch them.

"We wait and let that bitch Chelsea run herself blind while we play our position until someone kills her. Then I will be next for the crown. Plain and simple, Brian. Now get the fuck out," Susanna said seriously. She was ready for her alone time.

Brian left without any words because he knew Susanna better than anyone. She was bi-polar and could flip on you in a second.

***

Downtown Brooklyn

Tonight, was Gunna's birthday and he was turning twenty-two. NH and their crew were waiting for him in a new club next door to the Buzz night club.

Gunna was in his condo walk-in closet getting dressed in an all-white Dolce & Gabbana outfit, with four VVS rope chains on and his bust down diamond sky-dweller Rolex watch.

Zaby walked into the walk-in closet in her boy shorts and Hermes t-shirt barefooted leaning on the wall smiling.

"How do I look babe?" Gunna said looking at her reflection in the mirror.

"Good, handsome, sexy, swagged out on some Brooklyn shit," she said with her accent.

"You been hanging around me too long, babe," he said kissing her lips.

"Whatever birthday boy," she said touching his necklaces. The two been very serious with each other they both was in love and the happiest they ever been.

"You sure you don't want to come?" he asked.

"No go enjoy yourself. Clubs are not my thing. I'm from the Middle East. If they catch us in a club or house party, you get punished."

"This is Brooklyn. We do what the fuck we want."

"I know but I just want you to go enjoy yourself, birthday boy," she said walking away.

Gunna walked out the walk-in closet into their private master bedroom to see Zaby laying in their California King size bed under the Burberry sheets reading, *A Gangsta Qu'ran* from Lock Down Publications.

"I'ma hit you before I leave so you can get ready to get this birthday dick," Gunna said.

"I'm always ready for that," she added.

***

Hours later

The club was popping. Gunna and his Brooklyn team had the big VIP section sewed up as some scammers from Flatbush had the small VIP litty.

Gunna was saucy from Dom P and Henny. He was drunk but not sloppy drunk.

"Yo NH, we out, son. It's over you heard," Gunna said with a slur over the loud music as strippers ran around shaking their ass.

Gunna and his crew made it outside, almost falling down the stairs. Gunna caught himself as his seven men crew laughed.

Once in the lot, he fumbled in his pocket for his keys in as a gang of white boys with guns drawn hopped out of two Tahoe trucks with Chelsea. Gunna and her were face-to-face with guns pointed at him and his crew

Before she could even get a word out, shots rang out from the dark shadow, taking out her whole team with headshots, as Gunna's crew took cover.

Chelsea couldn't see the snipers, so she hopped in the SUV as her driver raced off. Gunna and his crew shot at the SUV, stepping over nine dead bodies.

Zaby stepped out the dark with an RPG assault rifle, dressed in all black as everybody was at a loss of words.

"I brought your Porsche. You want me to take the Audi, babe?" she said as Gunna's Brooklyn team stared at her.

"NH take my Porsche. Y'all good?" Gunna asked as everybody stared at Zaby with their mouths open as Gunna and Zaby hopped in his Audi, speeding off.

Romell Tukes

Chapter Sixteen

Abu Dhabi

"Sir As-salaam-alaikum," his main guard on the lower level stated into Zayid's earpiece as he was in his home office going over some business agreements.

"Wa-alaikum-salaam. Umar, what's going on?"

"You have a visitor by the name of Elena, sir and she came with a lot lot of security."

"Ok let her up alone," Zayid said taking his earpiece out, leaning back in his chair wondering what she wanted. It had been years since they saw each other.

Zayid and Elena's history went deep to nearly twenty years ago. He used to supply her and her family for years. Things got a little sexual between the two. They were seeing each other until they cut off the sexual relations because it was bad for business.

Five years ago, Elena started to grow her own coca leaves and plants to produce coke, thanks to Zayid teaching her everything she knew.

Zayid heard a knock at her door. It was one of his guards with Elena behind him in a black classy Salvatore Ferragamo satin dress with heels and her hair flat.

"Zayid, good to see you."

"You too, Elena. It seems as if you never age."

"Same for you too," she added showing her thirty-two pearl whites.

"How can I help you? I haven't heard from you in years. I hear you're doing pretty good for yourself."

"Somewhat, but I have a couple of questions. Do you know a man named Murda? The son of Web?"

"Uhmmm, no I've never heard of such a name."

"Oh yeah?" Elena said pulling four photos from her purse of Zayid and Murda entering a casino together side by side across town. "I'm very connected."

"I don't know who that is."

"Don't fucking play with me, Zayid," she yelled getting angry as her eyes turned red.

"Elena what do you want to know and why? I'm sure you don't need me to do research."

"Do you supply him?"

"Now that's none of your damn business, you low life," Zayid shouted.

"I guess that's a yes," she laughed.

"He's family and you know how I feel about family. You have a problem with him, then you have one with me," he replied seriously.

"I'm sure. I guess were done here. You said so much and so less of words."

"You know the door."

"Yes, I do. I've seen it so many times. Take care, Zayid. I'm sure I won't be seeing your handsome face again."

"Your threats don't faze me. Don't forget, I taught you everything you know," Zayid said honestly.

"I know, thank you." she said walking out smiling.

"Umar call the maid to bring my blood pressure medicine," Zayid said into his earpiece.

"Yes sir."

Zayid couldn't believe she had the nerve to come to his palace trying to get information out of him so she can use it on his client. He made a note to call Murda and let him know what he's up against if it's not too late.

He felt sad for Murda because he had big problems with the most dangerous women in the world. He had no clue what he did to piss these crazy bitches off.

The maid came in with two pills and a glass of water for him.

"Thank you," he said as the maid rushed out to go finish his halal lunch.

Seconds later, Zayid felt his heart racing as he grabbed his chest before his body went into shock. He died in his chair with blood pouring out his nose.

Elena knew Zayid's maid from years ago, so she had her goons kidnap her family until she agreed to switch Zayid's meds with some super deadly pills filled with rat poison and other deadly chemicals.

***

Rumson, NJ

Celine was in her mansion that she shared with her husband, Fernando. The mansion was 18,617 square foot, on 8.7 acres of land, containing seven bedrooms, four bathrooms, herringbone parquet flooring, a golf course, cherry doors, a pool, a dry sauna, a tanning room beside the exercise room, panorama windows and a boathouse.

This was their second mansion within a four-block radius. This mansion was worth $24.6 million, while their other mansion was $18.5 million and a little smaller.

Celine was a thirty-year-old beauty tall, skinny, a brunette, fake big double DD breasts, long sexy legs, wash board stomach, small butt, green eyes, big ears, and a tan complexion from all her tanning she did.

She was normally flying around the world on Fernando's private jet on shopping trip, vacations, clubs, or out with friends spending his money.

The only reason she married him was for his money because he wasn't her type at all.

Celine was raised in Princeton, New Jersey, an upper-class neighborhood with her parents who were German's from Berlin, Germany. Her parents were both bank owners and very successful.

Fernando was out golfing at his golf club, which gave her time to tan, swim, and exercise because when he was home, all he wanted to do was fuck, fuck, and fuck. When he was on the blue pill, it felt like his dick would stay hard for years, which pissed her off every time.

She was in the tanning room under the new tanning bed she recently brought, listening to a Drake song on her MP3 player and headphones, as she heard a loud thump sound, causing her to remove her headphones.

"Fernando, you're back?" she said lifting up the cover to the bed climbing out in her tiny Balmain two-piece bikini with her pussy lips hanging out with a long fold of extra skin that looked nasty.

As soon as she stepped out the tanning booth, she was met two guns to her face.

"Oh, my God, please! Fernando will be back any minute, please. I'll even call him," she told Gunna and Ariana.

"Bitch, shut up," Ariana said.

"Ok, ok please. I'll do whatever just don't kill me. I'll tell you all of his business locations," she begged.

"We already received everything from the office upstairs. We didn't even know you were in here until we heard you singing *God Plans*," Gunna said trying his hardest not to laugh because she couldn't sing for shit.

"You can't sing at all. That's what's about to get you killed. I guess it is God's plan," Ariana said shooting her twelve times in the face as chunks of meat flew everywhere.

Gunna tossed her body back into the tanning bed and turned the heat up to the maximum 450 degree, before they left the majesty mansion.

Chapter Seventeen

Brooklyn, NY

Eastern parkway was blocked off. Half of Brooklyn was shut down for the biggest parade of the year, Juve, which had the city of Brooklyn turned up for three days straight.

Juve was a West Indian parade filled with Trinidadians, Tobagonians, Caribbean's, Jamaicans, Barbadians, Bajans, Kittittiesans, Nevisians and Bahamians.

The streets were fill with women half naked dancing, fucking, singing, and enjoying the night. Everyone wore paint on their faces and body as a part of their outfits.

Loud music could be heard blocks ad blocks, away as groups of women, young and old danced down the streets to drums and music.

NH was half Trinidadian on his father side, so he would normally come to celebrate every year and tonight was no different. Tonight, he was turned up in his Gucci outfit drinking a blue cup fill of lean.

Tonight, was the last night and the whole Brooklyn came out. Every Crip in the city was out in their blue flags and island flags representing their culture and Caribbean backgrounds.

"Yo, cuz this shit moving out here boy," Fat Loc yelled as NH and his gang posted up on the corner with twenty females smoking and drinking with the loc's.

"Facts. I'm trying to see where the after party at cuz," NH said as a thick cute redbone chick pulled up to him and started to dance on him. She had a Tobagonian flag tied around her long dreads. "Damn ma you about to break a niggas dick," NH told the chick who was twerking on his dick in a bikini under a fish net dress showing her curves and big breast.

"I'm sorry daddy, but what's goody? You know what I'm trying do," she stopped dancing and told him showing her tongue ring.

"We about to get out of here anyway. This shit almost over ma," NH said as six NYPD officers walked past them patrolling the area to make sure there was no violence. Last year, there were five bodies that dropped due to gang violence at Juve.

"Let's go to club Lust. Shawty told me that shit going to be live tonight," 40 stated talking to two dark skin chicks with Jamaican flags looking like sisters.

"Aight," NH said as his crew and a gang of women walked up the crowded block. NH and his crew parked in a McDonald's parking lot because all the blocks were packed with cars.

"NH, where are we taking all these bitches?" Fat Loc rushed ahead of the crowd to whisper in his right-hand man ear.

"Nigga we're going take them to a hotel. What the fuck you think, Crip? They not coming to my cribs," NH said as the light skin chick on his arm heard him and sucked her teeth.

Once in the McDonalds parking lot, a U haul truck was blocking in NH's sky-blue McLaren 570s and Fat Loc BMW X5M SUV as well as two blue Benz G550 trucks that belonged to his crew.

"Who the fuck would block us in?" 40 shouted as the back door of the truck flew open and bullets ripped through his skull as a gang of shooters hopped out like the army with assault rifles spraying.

NH fired back overwhelmed as shooters continued to hop out the truck.

Tat!

Tat!

Tat!

Tat!

Tat!

Tat!

Tat!

The gunmen were taking out NH's crew one by one as everybody was running around in the parking lot, shooting or trying to dodge bullets.

"Shit," NH yelled using the now dead, redbone female as a shield.

NH saw a red Hellcat pull up within ten feet away from him, when he saw a sexy white chick hop out with an AK-47 with a hundred shot drum.

Gabby aired the parking lot out, killing twelve gunmen as everybody tried to run in the closest fast-food store. She caught the last one by shooting him three times in the back of the head.

"Get inside. Leave your car," Gabby said as NH followed her in her Hellcat to see all of his homies dead, especially Fat Loc who he grew up in the sandbox with.

***

Across Town

Murda and Jamika were both dressed to impress as they were out on their date, something they hadn't done since before their child was kidnapped.

The fancy restaurant was near a river front with a view of the Hudson River and the city of Manhattan across the bridge. The dim lights, candlelight setting, world class cooks, fancy rugs, leather chairs, wall paints, recessed upper windows on the second level, an inside and outside kitchen.

"Thank you for coming out and you look beautiful," Murda said looking into her sexy eyes. Her nice Louis Vuitton satin gown slit dress all black matching her LV heels. She also had LV logos on her manicured toes and nails.

"Anything for my sexy husband, but where is this damn food," Jamika laughed, drinking some expensive wine, leaving her red lipstick on the glass.

"It should be here, but how's work, babe? I been having so much going on lately, I've been slacking on being a husband."

"You're a great husband, trust me, but you having a lot going on wouldn't have to do with the city murder rate on the rise again, now would it?" she asked seriously knowing her husband would never lie to her.

The past couple of weeks she been getting reports from her boss about big shootouts, leaving people dead including civilians all over the city.

Her boss believed there is a new war forming under their nose. Why and with who was her job to find out.

"Jamika."

"Murda, you promised me you was done with this bullshit after what happened to our..." she paused unable to say because the loss of her son was still fresh on her mind.

"I know, but you don't understand what's going on."

"I don't? Are you fucking kidding me?" she said as their food arrived.

"He's back."

"Who?"

Stacks and I have a reason to believe our son is alive," he said as her face froze. "I have to catch him, baby. I didn't want to worry you because I'm trying catch up with him," Murda said as he saw her eyes well up with tears, but nothing fell.

"Get our son back," was all she said before they ate their meal with many thoughts running through both of their minds.

Chapter Eighteen

Abu Dhabi

Zaby just arrived in Dhabi after hearing about her father's death almost a week later. When her sister, Zainab called her in a sad voice, she knew it was serious.

Zaby had no clue who could or would kill her father, because he was always well protected by the best trained men in the Middle East and he was a great generous man.

Zayid had a lot of respect and power within his country and outside of his own country.

Looking out the limousine window, she felt weak as if she wanted to cry out loud, but she yearned for the person who caused this grief on her and her family.

She wore all black and her hijab to match her black garment to her father's Muslim funeral in a local mosque she grew up inside with Zainab.

***

Inside the packed mosque her father was having a traditional Islamic funeral. Zaby made her way to the front of the crowd to see her father in a casket wrapped in white sheets.

The body was placed on top of the shrouds and a mixture of perfume and camphor could be smelled.

The prayer was about to start as soon as the Imon walked out the back with Zainab as Zaby took a seat.

The Imon stood near the casket as everybody was behind him in prayer position.

"Allah Akbar. Allah Akbar. Allah Akbar. Allah Akbar," the Imom yelled then reciting the Al-fathah surah from the Qu'ran in Arabic. He stood parallel to the head of the deceased male.

Zayid's body was placed in the direction of the Qiblah, which was east. Sfter the prayer, the Muslim men dug a lahd, which wasa hole for his body out back where there was a large graveyard.

Hours later, Zainab and Zaby was in their father's mansion that he rarely went to because he normally stayed at his penthouse suite.

"What a day. How are you doing, sis?" Zainab asked her sister as she took off her hijab making her hair fall to her lower ass.

Zainab and Zaby looked very similar. It was hard to tell them apart because they were actually identical twins. Zainab was born seconds earlier the Zaby.

Zainab was a little thicker, with bigger C cup breast, and longer hair that almost touched the floor.

"Yeah I just wish I was here."

"Don't kill yourself, Zaby. We both had no control over what happened to daddy."

"I know I just feel like shit," Zaby said laying down on the couch.

"Daddy left us both a couple of billion dollars. The money should be in our accounts and he divided his properties amongst us both. He also left a letter. It's like he knew his time was coming and that freaks me out," Zainab said in her thick Arabic accent.

"This is crazy, Zainab. Who is prepared for death?" Zaby stated.

"He left me in charge of the family oil and drug trade. No wonder why he had been training me daily on the drug trade."

"Good."

"Good what? So, you're ok with me controlling the family drug and oil business?"

"Hell yeah. That's not my line of work. I'ma killer, Zainab."

"Ok but fifty percent of everything is yours, so you will be set for life."

"I'm in love, Zainab."

"What? Not you, Ms. 'I hate every man on earth'. Give me the tea," Zainab stated sitting next to her sister.

"He's Murda's little brother. I fell head over heels for him and he is such a good person."

"Isn't he the one who daddy told me about?"

"I believe so."

"Good, I'm supposed to be setting up meeting with all of my clients soon."

"Zainab, don't do nothing dumb." Zaby said looking at her seriously.

"Ok, I won't."

"I'ma look into who killed daddy before I leave," Zaby stated.

"No need to, sis. Follow me," Zainab said getting up walking downstairs to the basement filled with security guards.

When Zaby made it inside the back area of the oakwood floor basement, she saw her father's maid tied up in the corner crying.

"What does the maid have to do with daddy's death?"

"Tell her," Zainab told the lady who was scared to death. Zainab pulled out a pistol and the lady started to move her lips.

"Please, she forced me to switch his medicine. I didn't know what it was. She was going to kill my family," the maid cried.

"Who?" Zaby said with tears.

"The Spanish woman. Her name is Elena and I overheard her tell her guards on the phone she was going back to New York."

Zaby took Zainab's gun out of her hand and emptied the clip in the maid's body before walking off as the guards all got out her way.

***

Downtown Lower Eastside, NY

"How the fuck did you let that happen? We lost thirteen men. You know how this shit looks?" Silvio spazzed on his capo Jimmie in his lavish European expensive condo in the heart of downtown.

"It was fifteen men we lost, boss, but we had our main target. I was in the building watching the whole scene," Jimmie stated.

"So, what went wrong? I don't have time for slips, Jimmie. I'm supposed to be able to trust you and your judgement."

"I know boss but a woman pulled up in a Hellcat and took out my whole team, saving the kid and then police arrived seconds later on foot," Jimmie said rethinking about the event he watched from across the street.

It was a brilliant plan he came up with after Silvio gave him Gunna and NH's profile. He knew NH was Caribbean and would be at Juve and he also had his license plate to his McLaren.

The luxury car was easy to find. There weren't too many people driving around McLaren's.

"Try better next time, Jimmie. Tell Aunty I said hi," Silvio said dismissing him upset.

Jimmie was his twenty-six years old cousin from the hood part of Brooklyn. He was the only gangsta white boy in Glynwood.

He was 100% Italian, but he acted blacker than Wesley Snipes in Blade. Jimmie was the muscle to the Janeiro Crime family, even though he was built like a toothpick.

Chapter Nineteen

Colombia

Carmilla was horseback riding in horse field with her son in her lap, trying to teach him how to ride a horse since he had been begging her.

"Mommy I want to get down," Web Jr. cried as he held on to the straddle for dear life. The horse was going too fast for his taste.

"We just got on, baby. I got you just hold on," she said as the horse ran laps around the horse track barricades.

"Mommyyyy, I don't want to ride the horsey, no more," Web Jr. said in his kid tone, as she stopped the horse.

"Ok," Carmilla said climbing down and taking him down. She took off his helmet and hers and left to take him out for lunch.

She normally spent weekends with her son. While weekends she tried to balance both, which she been doing for years as a single mother.

Her guards follow them off the horse ranch where people came to ride horses and learn how to ride them.

"I don't like to see you quit. You're not a quitter. You're a big boy now, ok?" she told her son holding his little hands.

"I know mommy, but I don't like horsey's no more," he said mispronouncing the name, making her laugh.

"It's a horse baby."

"Oh."

"Let's go eat," Carmilla said as her guards opened the door for her and her son.

***

Mount Vernon, NY

"Damn, son. You just fucking really farted in a niggas face," Stacks said sitting in Black's living room as he walked past him passing gas.

"Nigga, it's my crib. What the fuck you mean?"

"Yeah aight nigga. Did you order that food?" Stacks asked his nephew while cleaning a load of guns on the living room table.

"I've been did that, son, but if the feds run up in here, I hope you taking all them charges. You know I'ma lose my section 8, so I hope you coming out them pockets when you in Valholla County Jail shit because I'm telling. I'm not built for jail, Unc. I'm sorry," Black said honestly shaking his head.

"I already know what type of nigga you are. It's no need to explain Black, but I'm about to slide soon, you heard."

"What you be doing all day in Brooklyn, son? I never see you no more," Black said playing games on his smart phone.

"None of your business. I won't let you give me to the feds."

"What are you trying to say? I'ma rat?"

"No, you haven't told. All I'm saying I know you would if given a chance in a tight spot," Stacks said cleaning off his last pistol placing it in a duffle bag.

"Whatever," Black said hearing the doorbell ring, which was the pizza man "Nigga answer the door, dummy," Stacks told his nephew who stood up and walked through his kitchen to answer his front door for the pizza man.

Stacks had been so busy planning tactics and trying to get a hold of Murda, he forgot about the baby. Elena was upset she was losing men, but their mission was getting closer and closer, so the risks and losses were well worth it. The two had been having sex daily. Stacks had to admit, Elena was a different type of bitch. He loved everything about her, but they were both too much alike, which scared him.

Stacks ate his pizza while his nephew talked and played the PlayStation 4 game system. He left and headed back to Brooklyn where he had his own low-key apartment then he planned to go visit Elena in Rye.

***

Brooklyn, NY

In a nice brownstone middle class neighborhood in Williamsburg, BK is where Silvio's mom lived at for thirty years.

"Uhmmmm," Cory moaned loudly as he watched Olivia bop her head up and down on his dick.

Olivia was sucking his dick slowly with her hands massaging his saggy, black balls as she went deep swallowing his black rod.

She made his dick disappear back and forth in her mouth until he finally came. She swallowed it, smiling with no teeth.

Olivia was fifty-five years old, thick, gray hair, big large breast she had done four times, wrinkles, but overall, she was still cute for an old woman. She had 100% Italian in her blood. She was a gangsta. She even did a jail bid before.

Her black neighbor Cory was a forty-year-old man who would come by daily to fuck her brains out and she would love it.

"Bend me over, big daddy," she said with her raspy voice as Cory put her on all fours. Her pussy was dry when he entered her, so he spit on his dick, spreading her soft ass cheeks apart ramming his dick in and out of her

"Ohhhh slow down," she jumped

Cory long stroked his dick in a motion hitting her G-spot as her big titties bounced back and forth against the sheets.

Her pussy was loose, but she was able to squeeze her pussy walls on his dick as he went deeper with a rhythm.

"Uggghh, fuck me with that nigger dick," she yelled as Cory started to fuck her like a rag doll. He slid his dick in her tiny asshole, as she screamed and cursed as she hadn't been fucking in her ass in years.

"Ohhh noooo. Ugh please," she moaned as he fucked her deep in her ass getting every inch.

"You love this nigga dick now?" Cory shouted sweating pounding out her asshole.

"Yesss I love it," she yelled.

Bloc!
Bloc!
Bloc!
Bloc!

Bloc!

Cory's body fell over Olivia as she tossed him off her, seeing he had blood pouring out his from five different holes.

"Ahhhh," Olivia yelled, when she realized what was going on. She locked eyes with Gabby.

"Hey," Gabby said pointing her gun at her.

"You fucking bitch! I was about to climax. Who are you?" Olivia said pissed off showing her bushy pussy.

"I'm looking for your son, Silvio."

"Well keep looking, bitch. You're fucking with the wrong family," Olivia yelled in her raspy voice, showing no fear. Catching a whiff of of a stench, she twisted her face before realizing the smell was coming from her pussy.

"Ok."

Bloc!
Bloc!
Bloc!
Bloc!
Bloc!
Bloc!
Bloc!

Gabby filled her upper torso with hot bullets, then she left laughing because the old white bitch had a vicious mouthpiece.

Chapter Twenty

Midtown, NY

Brian just walked out the clinic angry with medicine in his hand. Brian had eight small bumps on his upper lip, thanks to Susanna.

The doctor told him he had two different types of STD's and the only person he had any sexual intercourse with was Susanna, which was only oral sex and foreplay.

Normally he would have six guards with him at all times, but he was too embarrassed to walk into a clinic with his soldiers. He knew he would be the laughingstock of the family.

He climbed in his Uber texting Susanna informing her they had to talk ASAP.

"Take me to 39th West street," Brian told his black Uber driver as he pulled off the curb into rush hour traffic.

Brian was so pissed off. He wasn't even paying attention to the driver as he pulled into a build parking garage.

"Sir where are..." Brian said as he turned to the driver who stopped the truck and placed the biggest pistol in his face he ever saw in his life.

"Susanna, where is she?" Murda said as Brian laughed.

"I'm just as dead."

"Have it your way, my G."

BOOM!

BOOM!

BOOM!

Murda hopped out the truck and climbed in black Nissan GTR racing out the parking out lot.

Murda was watching Brian all morning since he got the drop on him. When he saw him waiting on a curb, he had a feeling he was waiting on a cab or Uber.

So, he tried his luck and pulled up in his black SUV with tints. Brian thought he was the Uber driver when he picked him up in Queens at his apartment.

Murda was on a mission to take out Chelsea's crew family by family and save her for last because he was a firm believer in a boss was only as good as they crew as Web taught him.

***

Abu Dhabi

Gunna walked up the stairs of the long entrance that lead to the architect 18th century French onyx style mansion with an impeccable landscaping.

Once inside, he was speechless by the marble floor, three levels a staircase with hand-forged wrought iron art, high fifty-foot ceiling, interior living space, and fancy expensive vases with fresh flowers inside.

"Follow me outside," one of the guards stated as Arabian men with assault rifles walked around in the house and outside.

Gunna was asked to come out here by Zainab personally. She spoke with Murda and he informed her Gunna would be handling all the business affairs and that was perfect for her.

Out back was beautiful hot, humidity, a L shaped swimming pool, a shooting range in the deep field, which stretched about twelve acres, an outdoor bar and kitchen with tables and chairs.

"Wow," Gunna said amazed.

"Gunna, hey! I'm Zainab," she said standing to face him in her Muslim garment, but she didn't have her beautiful face covered. Gunna was appalled by her beauty and presence because she looked like Zaby.

"Y'all twins?" Gunna asked.

"She didn't tell you?" Zainab laughed, knowing her sister hated telling people she had a twin.

"No but I'm sorry to hear about Zayid. I've heard so much good things about him."

"He was a great man. Thank you."

"This is a nice place."

"Yeah it's me and Zaby's. We have so many homes," she said. "Let's get down to business. How is the product moving?" she asked.

"That shit is the best work I've ever got. My people cutting that shit so much, the fiends want more. Cut the shit so strong, I'm running through one thousand keys in three days. I got people down south, the Midwest and on the Westcoast," he said.

"Good."

"Have you been receiving the payments?"

"Yes, everything is perfect. I will continue the same route my father took with shipment. The same prices, and quality," she stated.

"Great, perfect."

"Now that's out the way. My sister is really into you. She's never been in love. Please don't break her heart because she may really kill you," Zainab added laughing but serious.

"Love is a dangerous game, but I'm in love with her also and soon we'll all be one big family."

"Oh, is that right?" she said as she clapped her hands as a line of naked women came out the house in heels looking sexy. "These women are all for you. As they say in Vegas, what happens in Dhabi stays in Dhabi," Zainab said as the women rubbed their pussies and titties, ready to fuck.

"Thank you, but I'm ok. Thank you again for bringing me out, but I got to go. We have a lot going on back home," Gunna said paying the women no mind at all.

"Ok respect," Zainab said happy he passed the test because all of the women were sexy but HIV positive. This was one of Zainab's sick tests.

"I'll see you soon," he said standing to leave.

"Gunna you and my sister are perfect for each other. Be on the lookout for your shipment next week," she yelled to him.

***

Manhattan, NY

Elena was in a park early in the morning with four guards nearby, posted watching her exercise as she did every morning.

Elena was wearing MGF Gear as she ran the stairs in her tights, tank top, and Nike running shoes with her hair in a ponytail.

Days ago, she saw Brian on the news found dead in a truck inside of a garage. She felt sorry for him because that was some waste of some good soldiers. She ran up and down the stairs like the fitness junkie she was. This is what kept her body toned and pussy walls tight. With only one child, her pussy was very intact. She missed her daughter daily, but she knew she had to focus.

Elena had her headphones in her ear listen J.Balvin's album on her iPod. As she was running back down the stairs, she saw two of her guards drop as their head exploded.

Elena rushed to the top of the stairs and grabbed her Mack 11 she had under her MGF towel.

Tat!

Tat!

Tat!

Tat!

Her guards were shooting at the woman running across the field with a MP4 assault rifle.

Elena and Zaby were going shot for shot as Zaby shot another one of Elena's guards, leaving one standing.

"Get the car," Elena yelled, ducking and running from the bullets that shot off a chunk of her ponytail. "Bitch," Elena shot towards Zaby but missed her, as she climbed in Benz truck with her security guard racing off as bullets shattered her window.

Chapter Twenty-One

Bronx, NY

Gunna and his goons were outside in the back of a seafood restaurant in City Island waiting on the anonymous caller who called him informing him she had something very important to talk about.

Not thinking twice and being a businessman, he was willing to her the caller out.

"Yo Cutty, if them niggas move funny, take their head off, blood," Gunna told Cutty and his crew who was all surrounding the exit gate and the oceanfront rail looking into the water.

City Island was normally packed, but today wasn't nobody really out. Not to mention summer was almost over, so it was a little windy.

Gunna saw a woman in a white dress and fur coat. The woman was Spanish and beautiful, he couldn't deny the attraction.

She walked out back with eight men, matching Gunna's goons.

"I assume you're Gunna," Carmilla asked with a beautiful smile as her skin glowed off the little sun that was out today.

"I assume you're Ms. Anonymous," he replied taking a sip of soda, looking into the water as she sat down.

"I'm Carmilla. I'm the boss of the Colombia Cartel," she said as he finally looked her in her eyes.

"Ok and what does that mean?" he stated rudely.

"It means what it sounds like. I'm about business. That's why I contacted you," she shot back, not feeling his attitude are energy at all.

"You got five minutes. Better yet three," he said taking a loud slurp from his straw in his soda.

Carmilla was really trying to be patient because she knew he was young, so she tried her best to hold it together.

"I've done my research on you and your crew. I'm impressed. You have New York under your chin and in your palms."

"I don't know where you get your information from, but you should redo your research."

"I have the best coke and South American and I need your help to move it. I will front you twenty-five tons on consignment and then we can see more money than we've ever seen."

"Let me think about it. Uhmmm, no," Gunna stated, remaining loyal to his plug who just shipped him the mother load days ago.

"Are you sure this is what you want to do?" she asked with a smirk as he got serious.

"Bitch what the fuck you mean by that?" he yelled as his goons tensed up as well as her men.

"Would you call your mother a bitch? You're about to miss out on something big."

"I'll pass, bitch."

"Ok, have it your way. Just know regardless, I will conquer your areas with ease. Why make enemies when you can make friends?" she said standing to leave.

"You one lucky bitch," he said wondering how she found him.

"I'm only going to be some many bitches, papi," she said leaving as her goons followed as Gunna tossed his food and soda into the water.

***

Manhattan, NY

Chrissy had a long day at work as a police officer in the 72nd Precinct in the heart of Manhattan.

She did four drug raids today in Washington Heights and one of them it turned into shootout, killing one of her fellow NYPD officers.

At forty, she was black and beautiful fitness, dark-skin, neat dread, curves, classy and smart. She was 100% Trinidadian and raised in the crazy Flatbush section of Brooklyn.

She been a cop for fifteen years and she loved her job. She did it to protect and serve, unlike most dirty low-down cops on her force who dreamed of killing black men and kids.

Every time she arrested young men, she imagined it was her only son she was arresting, but she taught him well. Unfortunately, he chose the streets instead of the college life.

Chrissy loved her son, NH, but the life he lived she hated, she prayed for him daily.

It was 11pm and it was time to switch shifts and time for her to go home. She walked to her navy-blue new Benz E-class E four door sedan.

She pulled out the lot and made it two blocks away from her job before a Porsche Panamera pulled up on to the side of her and opened fire.

Chrissy was slumped over in her seat dead before the light could turn green. Susanna raced off in the Porsche, hearing sirens behind her blocks away.

***

Brooklyn, NY

NH was getting some head in his sky-blue Lambo outside of his apartment on Church Ave.

Cara was sucking the skin of his dick. She sucked the tip, making all types of noises as her pre-cum soaked his seats.

Cara was a dark-brown skin boney chick with a cute face, and crazy head game. She was Jamaican and loved sucking dick.

"Uhmmmm, nut in my mouth. I'ma catch it," she moaned bopping her head faster on his dick. He came, pushing her head all the way down on his dick as she took it down her throat.

The block was ghost town tonight, so nobody was out. Not that Cara cared anyway. She fucked and sucked half the hood off in broad daylight many times.

NH phone rang. It was his aunty. When he answered, she was crying. When she informed him, his mom was dead at the Brooklyn hospital, he felt as if he was in the twilight zone as he hung up.

"Get the fuck out."

"It's like that? I just swallowed all your nasty as nut. You know I don't swallow. I thought you was taking me inside your crib," she cried until he pulled out his gun. "Ok I'm gone," she said rushing out the Lambo.

NH quickly made his way to the hospital praying his mom was good and his aunty was over dramatic as she always was.

***

Augusta, Maine

Fernando was at a ski resort with a side chick named, Dakota who was a cute, short, slim, short hair woman. Dakota was a forty-three-year-old divorced white woman who was an ex-porn star, so she was very freaky.

The two been fucking all day but now they were under the blanket in front of the stone fireplace in the living room watching TV on the couch.

Since his wife's murder, he had been hiding in Maine. Chelsea started a war with the wrong people. He would watch the news and know it was Chelsea and Murda's work. He loved his life too much to risk it for nothing, so he was laying low until shit died down.

Chapter Twenty-Two

Manhattan, NY

Gabby was in her apartment watching a show on HGTV in her furnished living room. The place was hooked up. Luckily, she brought it like this two weeks ago.

The apartment was a skyrise, three bedrooms, two bathrooms, his/her's walk-in closet, a dining area, which opened to a balcony and two separate living room areas. Downstairs of the building there was an indoor pool, exercise area, library, computer room and a bar for the residents.

The place costed her $5,961 a month. It was better than her last location but the only thing that rubbed Gabby the wrong way was her new neighbor whom she hadn't seen.

For the past two-nights, Gabby been hearing moans, screams, cries, headboard banging, and weird sounds. Her neighbor had company all hours of the night. She planned to talk to whoever lived there some time this weekend.

Gabby had been trying to tail Murda and Gunna because she knew they would bring her Chelsea, but they had so much beef, everybody was at coming for them.

Gabby planned to go out to eat tonight and get some air. She hated being locked in the house all hours of the day.

She went to her master bedroom suite and got dressed in a Fendi outfit with some heels. She placed her long blonde hair in a ponytail and grabbed her 9mm Glock with a long thirty round clip hanging from the handle.

Once she exited her apartment, she made her way to the building elevator to hear people coming out the stairwell.

There were only four apartments on the floor and one apartment was empty and the other belonged to an old couple who were always on vacation, so she knew it was her neighbor.

Gabby waited for the elevator as she heard a woman yelling at two men, but she tried to mind her business.

"Excuse me Ms. Ms., you must be my quiet neighbor," a female voice said as Gabby turned around with a fake smile wondering if this was a fine time to tell her about the noise.

When Gabby saw who it was, she got cold feet. Her heart paused with angry, pain, and hurt.

Chelsea looked at Gabby and a weird feeling came over her. This was the first time the women were face to face. "You ok?" Chelsea asked seeing an awkward look on Gabby's face. Chelsea's guards sensed something was about to pop.

Gabby pulled out her gun and shot Chelsea in her left shoulder as the shootout started. Chelsea shot at Gabby, missing as one of the guards caught a head shot. Gabby hide on the side of the hallway wall.

Guards rushed out of Chelsea's apartment deep, shooting at the end of the hall where Gabby was waiting on the elevator.

Boc!

Boc!

Boc!

Boc!

Boc!

Boc!

Boc!

Boc!

Gabby dropped three of the guards as they shot back, putting holes in the wall near her head.

"Come on elevator," Gabby said as the shots from the high-powered rifles was turning the hallway into a shooting rang.

Gabby pulled out a gas bomb from her purse and tossed it down the hall as the elevator opened.

When she heard the guards coughing, she fired off some rounds and ran in the elevator as bullets ripped through the closing elevator doors. Gabby pushed the lower garage button to get to her car as she was upset from missing her target. She couldn't believe it was Chelsea the whole time living next door to her. She cursed herself for not being more cautious.

Gabby had so many pictures of Chelsea she could pick her out in Times Square on New Year's Eve, but it was oblivious Chelsea had no clue who she was, which she could've used to her advantage.

Once in her Hellcat, she raced through the city streets, lucky she had nothing important in that apartment, so she had nothing to worry about.

***

Nyack, NY

Jamika was sleep in her mansion, enjoying a nap on her day off as Murda went out to handle some business with his crew.

Murda been rolling around with a six-man crew and he begged Jamika to do so too, but she refused. She was an FBI agent, so running around with a crew of criminals would've alerted her co-workers and could end her career.

Since hearing her son could be alive, Jamika's mind had been racing and in overdrive. She wanted her baby back.

"Jamikaaa. Jamikaaa," a soft voice whispered, waking her up

"Baby you back early?" she said half sleep turning around under her covers to see a tall black nigga standing over her. "Oh, my God!" Jamika screamed, jumping up to see a pistol pointed at her.

"Bitch lay back down," Stacks said in a scary tone as she did just that.

"Stacks why? Where is my child? Please."

"Don't cry now. You were laughing, smiling and moved on when you thought I was dead. Now look at you," Stacks said with an evil grin.

"You're taking this too far. Is my son still alive?"

"Of course. He is beautiful," Stacks said closing in on her, rubbing her face then smelling her neck, making her feel uneasy. "I bet that pussy still good," he laughed.

"I just want my son. I'll do whatever please," she begged with tears.

"Maybe next time I'll take you up on that after, but I'ma go before your husband comes back. Let him know I'll see him soon. I should kill you, but you're a pawn on my chessboard, love," Stacks said leaving the same way he came in.

Jamika called Murda when she heard the downstairs door slam and he informed her to go in the panic room until he got there.

***

Forty-five minutes later.

Murda searched the whole house with his crew for any signs of Stacks. He couldn't believe he found out where he laid his head. He was slipping big time.

"Babe we're moving out of here tonight. Pack your shit," he said walking into the room to see her zoned out with tears rolling down her beautiful face.

"He said our son is alive," she said staring at the wall playing with her fingers.

"I'ma get our son back. It just takes time."

"How much time do you need, Murda? This is our son were talking about here," she added.

"I know but take into consideration the type of people we're dealing with. It will all work out, trust me," he said kissing her stiff lips. "You ok? He didn't touch you or nothing?"

"I'm ok. I just want Andrew back," she said getting up walking to the bathroom, slamming the door behind her.

Murda had to do something quick because he felt like the walls was closing in on him and Jamika was blaming him for this whole situation. He had to make it right.

Chapter Twenty-Three

Dix Hills, Long Island
Months later

"Why do I have to wear a blindfold? What if something pops off?" Zaby said dressed in a nice, tight off-white red and black dress with heels showing a little skin with her perfect curves.

"Don't worry about that. Lucci and a crew behind us," Gunna said laughing as the new white Wraith Black Badge Edition Zaby brought for him sailed through the gated community.

The past few months been an all-out war with Chelsea, Elena, and the Mob families. A lot of blood had been drawn in the streets. On the flip side, Gunna was making so much money, he ain't know what to do with it.

"We're here, love," Gunna said as Darnell Jones played in the surround sound system while the Wraith drove up the stone-paved driveway.

"Can I please take this stupid thing off now?"

"No," he said parking next to the eight-car garage as he hopped out and opened the door for her like a true gentleman. Zaby changed Gunna in so many ways. It was as if he turned into a man overnight.

Gunna took her blind off and when she saw the mansion, she wanted to cry because it was exactly how she describe her dream to him.

"Oh, my God! Wow baby. I can't believe you found it," she said amazed looking at the Tashdal style-built home with two water fountains in the front, glass doors, and a pink Wraith that matched his.

"That's your Wraith. Now you can match my fly."

"Thank you. Let's go inside."

Inside, the first thing they saw was a baccarat chandelier, massive iron and glass doors lies on expensive foyer with twin circular marble staircases going up three levels.

"Damn," Zaby said walking on the marble floor looking at the fifty-foot concilege, coffered ceilings as they walked into the spacious living room with white carpeting.

"I knew you would like it."

"Oh shit! Look at this backyard!" Zaby said walking through the stainless-steel top of the line gourmet kitchen towards the backyard.

The back had outdoor grills, a private lounge, a wet bar, two swimming pools, a basketball court, a shooting range, a bathhouse, and a garden.

The palace was 21,771 square feet, and contained twelve bedrooms, eight bathrooms, a movie theater, a gym, three walk-in closets, an elevator, two home official offices, and a panic room recently installed in the basement.

"You did your thing. I love it," she boasted.

"Good, but I just want to know if you will marry me?" Gunna said getting down on one knee pulling out a box with a big diamond ring worth $9.5 million dollars.

"Gunna this is crazy. Ohhh," she said covering her mouth as tears drenched the makeup off her face.

"Will you?"

"Yess fuck yeah nigga," she shouted hugging and kissing him as the toured the new house with his crew admiring their new chill spot.

***

Weeks Later

Zaby and Gunna got married in a big mosque by an Imam from Yonkers, NY. The mosque was filled with guest, mostly all Brooklyn niggas in downtown Brooklyn.

"Bro I'm so happy for you," Murda said as he talked to his brother who was rocking a nice tuxedo with a tie and a pair of black Stacey Adams.

"Good looks, son. I know she the one I'm ready to spend the rest of my life with," Gunna said watching Zaby talk to Jamika and a group of other women. She looked like an angel in her white long bride dress.

"I'm proud of you."

"How's things with you and Jamika?"

"To be honest, rocky bro. Ever since Stacks showed back up, I gotta find my son. This shit doesn't even feel real," Murda said. He was honestly losing a lot of sleep due to the disappearance of his son.

"I feel you. We're going take care of all them niggas. They just killed Ruff and Pob the other night, Silvio and his crew," Gunna said drinking Dom P.

"I heard but go on your honeymoon. Have fun. We'll handle that shit when you touch down. Go dance with your wife," Murda said as a Jagged Edge song blured through the speakers.

Murda saw Gunna and Zaby slow dancing as a crowd formed around them.

"Can I get a dance handsome?"

"I don't think my beautiful wife would like that."

"She'll be okay," Jamika said grabbing his hand to dance as she was alittle tipsy.

The night was a blast. Every enjoyed themselves and partied to celebrate the new love.

***

Panama City, Panama
Two days later

Gunna and Zaby had just gotten off the private jet to see a Rolls Royce limo waiting on them as Gunna ordered.

Zaby saw the beautiful mountain tops, and pine and coconut trees everywhere. The tropical climate heat beamed on their skin.

"This place is nice, but I wonder how far it is the Island?"

"I don't know," Zaby as the driver of the limo took their bags and placed them in the trunk.

It was Zaby's idea of coming to Panama while Gunna choice was Thailand for their honeymoon.

The driver and Zaby spoke in Spanish because Gunna didn't know a lick of Spanish.

"Get in come on baby," Zaby said as she climbed inside. They rode through Panama City, which looked like Manhattan with its tall skyrises revolutionize luxury builds.

They rode in the limousine for an hour until they had to get on a small boat heading to their private Island in Isla Poridita, near the city of Cocile.

Once they made it to the white sandy beach on the Island, they were both overwhelmed with the tropical foliage and coconut graves all set on the mountains backdrop and a small forest. The resort was 34,000 square feet made from rare tropical wood and glass the place was one of a kind private resort.

In their suite, their glass floors with a aquarium under it with whales, sharks, and sealions swimming around.

"I hope they can't get inside this bitch," Gunna said, looking at the shark's swim under his feet.

The luxury suite was bright with a sunken lava bathtub, library, Polynesian art and artifacts, crafted furniture, two master suites, an inside pool area, and an elevator leading to the upper second level.

"Let's go check out the rooms," Zaby said walking down the hall to see a master suite with the biggest bed they ever seen with a screen surrounding it. Everything in the room was all white, as the balcony led to the outback entertainment area used for party's and events.

"Thank you."

"For what babe?"

"Your love. Now I want to show you how much I love you," she said dropping to her knees, undoing his Gucci belt, pulled his pants down to meet with his raising big dick as she placed it in her mouth. She slowly sucked the tip, while humming as she worked her neck, engulfing his entire cock as she went up and down twisting her head, while doing tongue tricks as his knees almost buckled out on him.

When she felt his load about to erupt, she stopped and laid him down, taking off his clothes as he let her do her thing. She took off her dress exposing her little perky breast while she climbed on his dick riding it like a wild cowgirl.

"Ugh, fuck yeah," she yelled bouncing up and down on his dick. He parted her tight walls as he guided her waist down making her ass clap on his thighs every time she came down.

Her pussy was warm and dripping wet, as her natural tight pussy clenched his dick.

"I'm cumming," she moaned kissing him as he rammed his dick in and out of her until they both climaxed.

Gunna fucked her body upside down like a folding chair and fucked her doggy-style with his thumb in her asshole preparing it for later. Gunna fucked her in the air after that, as she rode his dick like a horse.

They fucked for six hours in every position known to man. They even made some shit up along the way. Gunna ate her pussy so good, as she yelled gospel songs, scaring the sharks away under their room floor.

The next couple of days was fun and full of joy. They went swimming with sharks and whales, fishing, boat riding, kayaking, hiking on the jungle trails filled with wildlife.

The employees at the resort catered to their needs. They also brought him and Zaby a lot of gifts, mostly jewelry.

Gunna knew jewelry and the jewelry they were receiving was worth millions, so when he told Zaby to inquire in Spanish where the gifts coming from, they told her the Panama Cartel. They were the most powerful organization on Central American boarder.

They informed them it's their job to make their time in Panama the best or their life could depend on it.

Gunna didn't have a clue who was the Panama Cartel, but he wanted to know how they knew him and his wife, but he would save that for another day.

He never saw Zaby so happy and relaxed, just as he was. They were having sex in public, at restaurants, on the beach, on a boat, in the water, and then even made love in a jungle where they saw Jaguars watching closely.

Chapter Twenty-Four

Williamsburg, Brooklyn

Jimmie pulled into Jenna's parking lot, dropping her off at her building in the nice Brownstone middle class neighborhood fill of Jewish people.

He was just coming back from taking his girlfriend on a date downtown at the Gotom Bar and Grill, which had the best grilled food in the city.

This was the only time he got to spend with Jenna in weeks because the beef with Murda and his goons were in a war zone. In an hour, he was supposed to meet with some of his trusted soldiers and plot some blueprints out on how to catch Murda.

"You not coming up? It's bad enough I haven't saw you in over a month, Jimmie and you know I'm horny and I miss you," Jenna said rubbing his leg licking her lips.

Jenna was a beautiful white woman, who was thirty-two years old, raised in a Jewish household. She worked as a licensed nurse in the Brooklyn hospital. She was tall, dark brown curly hair, long eyelashes, a big noise, cute face, slim frame, big breast, nice smile, and some good tight pussy, but her head game was sensual.

Jimmie checked his Patek Phillippe 5970 yellow gold watch realizing he had time to spare.

"You want to go upstairs?"

"No, I see my roommate is still up," Jenna said looking up at her apartment windows to see all the lights on as the rain poured down on the gray new BMW i8 with tints.

"So what you want to do?" Jimmie said as she smiled and leaned in his lap, pulling down his Dickies. She wasted no time in sucking him off until his medium sized, pink dick got hard.

Once hard, Jenna deep throated him with every gulp until tears formed in her eyes as she sucked his dick in a fast motion.

Jimmie was moaning as his face tightened. He looked in his rearview mirror to see a figure in a hoodie creeping up on his car slowly in the pouring rain with a gun.

Before he could even grab his gun, the gunmen was firing shots into his driver side window killing Jenna and him.

Murda ran down the block in the rain, almost slipping off the curb trying to hop in his black Ford Mustang Shelby GT 500.

Murda had been on Jimmie for a week now and normally, he had soldiers with him on his daily travels, but tonight was the perfect setting.

He wanted to kill Jimmie outside of the restaurant, but the parking lot was jammed pack. Murda had been hunting Chelsea's Mob families down one by one, but he was losing a lot of men every time they struck back. However, his plan was coming together.

***

South Boston, MA

The suburbs of Boston were blocks away from the ghetto and slums, but it still felt like a different world.

Gabby's cousin Missey was raised in the heart of the city with her Italian family, who was known for their pizza shops and gruesome wars with the Irish Mob.

Missey was in her two-story home feeding Gabby's daughter before she put her to sleep so she could do some shopping online.

Missey worked at home as a website designer and an author, so babysitting wasn't a problem. She wasn't too much worried about how long she would be babysitting. She was more so worried about what Gabby was up to.

Missey's doorbell rang twice as she got up with the baby in her arms, sucking on the baby bottle getting tired.

She didn't have no kids, but she always wanted one, but first she would have to find a man and she wasn't cute by far. Missey was fat, weighing in at two hundred and fifty pounds, ugly, pale skin, and with a lot of health problems.

Company this late was rare for her. The only people who came by daily was her brother, uncle, two best friends and her mom, but she thought Gabby was finally coming back to get her daughter.

"Hello," Missey said opening the door to see a very attractive white woman standing in front of two large men. They looked as if they were up to no good.

"Sorry to bother you but I'm with Children Protective Services. Gabby informed me her child was here," Chelsea said as Missey's face screwed up.

"Excuse me? This must be a mistake. She asked me to watch her daughter."

"I understand, but I guess she reported her child missing," Chelsea said as Missey's face went in shock.

"This can't be happening."

"Do you know where she is or how to reach her?" Chelsea asked.

"Uhmm no she just dropped him off. I don't even have a number for her. I'm going to be in trouble or going to jail."

"No, a little worse." Chelsea said pulling out a pistol, shooting Missey in the face and then the baby with no remorse. "That was a waste of time," Chelsea said walking down the walkway to the SUV as her guard was silent thinking about the event that just look place.

Killing kids was never allowed in the Mob until Chelsea took over. She made her own rules.

***

Putnam Valley, NY

NH was sitting in his BMW M4 CS watching the mini mansion across the street with the manicured lawn and three car garages filled with Harley Davidson bikes.

It was midnight and pitch black on the block, as NH was waited on his target who should be here within minutes like clockwork.

Last week was the hardest moment of his young life because he had to bury his mother. The funeral was filled with cops and detectives to mourn and grieve over their fallen officer who services their city well.

At the funeral, NH saw a familiar face with the chief of police. The familiar face was Susanna, the woman who ran the Cavallari Family. Gunna had shown him pictures of all the family bosses and capo's just so he knew who was who.

When he saw her, it wasn't hard to put the connections together of who was responsible for his mother's death.

NH did some research that day and asked a couple of cops who the beautiful woman was with the chef of police and they told him she was his daughter, who was a restaurant owner, but NH knew better.

The chief of police pulled into the driveway in a Ford-150 pickup truck, just getting off work and drained.

Mr. Cavallari was an old biker boy. He loved to ride. That was his life outside of work. He was different from his crazy brother was running the family Mafia.

He tried to raise his kids outside the Mob life, but it was just in their blood, but he stayed from away from it.

The other day he had dinner with his daughter and informed her about all the brutal events that had been going on in the city. She denied any parts, but she did mention a name that he had his lieutenant look into.

He climbed out his truck with his work bag before walking into his garage, which was normally open as his wife was inside waiting on his arrival as she did every night.

"Heyyyyy," a voice shouted as Cavallari looked back.

Bloc!
Bloc!
Bloc!
Bloc!
Bloc!
Bloc!
Bloc!

Bloc!

NH shot the old man in his head, face, and neck, avoiding the bulletproof vest he had on. When he saw the man's bloody body collapse at the door entrance, he took off.

Chapter Twenty-Five

Lower Westside, NY
Weeks later

Gabby watched the building where Silvio worked closely as the two guards in the lobby were preparing to change shifts with the overnight lobby guards. Silvio was upstairs doing overtime.

She recently got back from Boston where she buried her daughter, which was hard to do, but she had to remain strong.

When Gabby got the call from her cousin that Missey and her daughter was killed, she felt as if the world ended. Now with nothing to live for, Gabby was going the extra mile to ruin Chelsea's army and puppets until she caught up with the boss herself.

Gabby spent hours studying Silvio's movement and the only way to kill him was at work because his home was guarded 24/7 and he also kept guards in the garage of main office.

The only thing that could fill her heart and offer some peace, was killing and that was her goal right now as she climbed out the Hellcat and walked across the street. The new guards were now setting up there workplace as the other two gay guards were driving home together for a long night of hot steamy rough sex.

***

"This asshole doing overtime again," one of the guards said leaning back in the seat.

"Yeah, this cocksucker is so rich, I don't see why he needs to work. Did you see his Aston Martin in the garage?" a short fat white man said to the tall young black lobby guard.

"Yeah that shit is fly," the black guard said as he saw a sexy blonde chick walk in the building.

"Ms. I'm sorry, but we're closed," the fat white man stated, doing his job because nobody was allowed in the building after ten at night except Silvio.

"I'm looking for my lawyer. He told me to meet him here," Gabby said as both men eyed her curves in her Louis Vuitton bodycon suit.

"Who may that be, beautiful?" the black guard said in a flirt tone, as she went in her purse to grab a piece of paper they thought.

Gabby pulled out a colt 45 with a silencer attached to it and shot both men in the center of their head.

She walked down the hall with her gun in her hand. Before she even made it halfway down the hallway of the fancy building lobby, six guards came out the elevator leaving their boss' office.

When the guards saw Gabby with a gun, they all reached for their weapons until the stairwell door flew open.

PSST!
PSST!
PSST!
PSST!
PSST!
PSST!
PSST!
PSST!
PSST!

The gunman with the RPG assault rifle also had a silencer and knife attached to the barrel.

Gabby saw all six guards laid dead on a pile near the elevator as her and the shooter made eye contact, both knowing who each other was.

"I guess we're here on the same mission. Follow me," Zaby said going upstairs in the stairwell to the level Silvio was on.

Gabby saw her dressed up like a ninja, wondering how did she get in the building, but however she did, she was glad because if she would of gotten into a shootout with the guards, the noise would of alerted Silvio and blew her cover.

***

Silvio was preparing for trial tomorrow for one of his wealthier clients, so he had to pull a double to make his opening statement and his closing argument.

He just sent his goons to patrol the area outside while he was in his office. There was a big war, and he wasn't getting caught slipping like his nephew Jimmie, who got caught with his pants down. His mother's murder hurt him the most.

Silvio came up with a plan to fish Murda in, but he would need Chelsea's help. He planned to speak to her about it this weekend to hear her insight because Murda was becoming a bigger problem than he thought.

"Ahhhh someone is hard at work," Gabby said with her gun aimed on him as well as Zaby assault rifle. He leaned back with his hands in the air.

"Wow they sent two sexy women to kill me? I never thought I'd see the day. Fuck the both of you, dirty bitches," he spit upset.

"You're just like your mother. She had a lot to say before I killed her too," Gabby said.

"You think you fucking smart..."

PSST!

PSST!

PSST!

PSST!

PSST!

PSST!

PSST!

Zaby filled his upper body with bullets as his body jerked with every hit from the powerful bullets.

"He talks too much," Zaby stated.

"I agree. You hungry?" Gabby said walking out the office.

"Sure! It's finally nice to meet you," Zaby told her as both women talked and walked down the carpet wall to wall floor.

***

Brooklyn, NY

It was an early snowy morning on Christmas and Elena was walking through the Pink House Projects alone in a hoodie and cargo pants, trying her best to look like a Spanish hood rat to fit in.

She walked in the building that looked disgusting, but smelled worse, as she took the elevator to the third floor.

Elena wanted to know where Murda's son was at, but Stacks refused to tell her. Even after weeks of fucking and sucking him, he still kept in a secret.

Not being one for secrets or games, she had her goon follow him from Mount Vernon to here, three times a week.

She knocked on the apartment door lightly and a woman opened the door with gray hair and a pretty face.

"Ms. Sanders?" Elena asked with her strong Spanish accent.

"Yes, who are you?"

"Your worst nightmare, bitch," Elena said pulling out a 9mm, shooting Ms. Sanders three times in her face as she ran in the old fashion apartment room to room.

The last room was a jackpot for Elena as she saw a baby boy playing with toys on the floor in diapers. He was so cute.

Elena went over to him as he looked at her oddly. She got on her knees and wrapped her hands around his little neck and started to choke him to death.

Lil Andrew's eyes almost popped out his eye socket as his face turned blue before he died. Elena smiled as she picked him up like a baby needing attention.

Elena opened the window as snow and strong wind blow into the room, she threw the baby body out the window. She left the building feeling as if she could finally let her daughter Teresa rest in peace now.

***

Downtown Brooklyn, NY

Carmilla had two condos in Brooklyn, but her new apartment had so many things wrong with it, she was considering moving.

She been in Brooklyn for a while now. She was on a mission to build a team of hustlers to take over Gunna's empire. Everybody she was coming across either worked for Gunna or a dude name NH or they were nervous, thinking she was the feds.

It was too much money in New York to walk away and she refused to go back to Colombia until she at least had half of Brooklyn buying bricks from her.

She brought a condo for her guards downstairs, but she normally kept four in her condo since there was five rooms, four bathrooms, his/hers walk-in closets, a view of the city, a large dining room, game room, a high ceilings,, cherry oakwood floors upstairs and downstairs, Italian cabinets, flat screen TVs all over the living room, a chef kitchen with high quality equipment and a state of the art surround sound system throughout the house.

Carmilla was in her room getting dressed for her evening. She had plans to meet a Puerto Rican dude from the Bronx, who had the Bronx on lock with coke, but word was he needed a new plug, so she was setting up a meeting with him.

Carmilla had her men shoot up six of Gunna's traps, killing seventeen of his goons and leaving his most profitable blocks hot as police shut his traps down and locked up his goons and workers.

It was all a part of her plan to divide and conquer. His success turning it into hers.

She heard her guards let the workers in as she been waiting for since she moved in.

Carmilla walked out her master bedroom in a white blouse and white jeans made by Dolce & Gabbana, with a pistol in her D&G purse. She put on her D&G sunglasses and put on her white Raf Simons fur coat because it was snowing heavy in New York.

"They finally came," Carmilla said to her guards as she made it downstairs to see two black men in blue jumpsuits with hats fixing her fireplace.

"They should be done soon, they said," one of the guards said as he looked at her phat pussy poking out her pants.

"Now Mikey, I told you before, it's not cute to stare at a lady's pussy. It makes you look like a creep," she said walking past him, about to leave until she saw one of the worker's face. Before she could even react Gunna and NH jumped up with Dracos spraying rounds at her guards and her.

Carmilla shot back hitting NH in his leg as Gunna tried to take her head off. She back paddled out the door, leaving her guards to fight because she was out of bullets.

By the time they killed four of her guards, they knew she was long gone as they ran downstairs and outside to see two SUV's Tahoe trucks and a Rolls Royce Dawn coupe all black speeding down the block.

"Shit," Gunna shouted fucking steaming at the fact that she got away.

Since Gunna been back from his honeymoon, someone been hitting his spots killing his men and he knew it was Carmilla. He was able to find her easily because she had the same Rolls Royce Dawn, he saw the first day they met. His goon tailed her one day to her condo.

"Bro I'm bleeding bad, son. I gotta get to Landon Ave. My cousin can fix me up," NH said as the climbed in a stolen Honda.

"Aight crybaby. How you let that bitch shoot you?" Gunna said pulling off still mad he missed his shot.

"Nigga didn't you get shot by a bitch?" NH cried in pain as Gunna laughed.

Chapter Twenty-Six

Mount Vernon, NY

NH was in a lounge and bar celebrating his birthday with a couple of Crips from Brooklyn, drinking and talking shit, enjoying the night

The lounge had two VIP sections, a DJ booth, stage, dance floor, two bars, and a mixture of bartenders from Spanish to white.

This was the first time NH had been out in a while, especially after his mom's murder, but he knew he would need some time to heal.

"Where them bottles at son?" Mead yelled already drunk from the bottle of Henny he already gulped

"Nigga sit your drunk ass down," P.O.G told his friend, as he was standing on the couch looking for one of the sexy bartenders.

"This spot fake litty," NH said as he saw the dance floor packed with couples dancing and niggas and bitches trying to choose.

"I'm so sorry for the wait, gentlemen," a sexy white chick said approaching their table in boy short showing her nice tone legs and phat pussy. Her work shirt was cut in half, showing her flat stomach as her titties sat up nice as she dropped of eight bottles of Ace of Spade on a cart and four big bottles of Henny.

"It's cool sexy," NH said staring at her beautiful face. She was the baddest bitch he saw all night.

"You must be the birthday boy," she said catching his sexual eye contact and delivering her own back to him. She eyed his blue American Apparel sweatsuit with his two Cuban link chains' hanging from his neck.

"Yeah and you must be my birthday gift," NH said making her blush, showing her beautiful smile and dimples

"Nigga that shit was lame. I'ma show ya how to do it. Yo, ma, I'm trying to fuck," Mead yelled with his buck teeth making everybody laugh except the bartender.

"I would never fuck you, yuck mouth," she said walking off as NH got up to stop her.

"Look ma, I'm sorry about that, but I'm trying spend some time with you. How about you give me your number and we get up tomorrow?" NH said looking into her cat eyes.

"You better call me," she said giving him her number and name Margaret.

NH was about to go back to the VIP, but the Ace of Spade had him ready to piss every ten minutes, so he made his way to the restroom.

Inside the restroom, NH saw a dark-skin nigga washing his hands dressed in a fly ass Balmain outfit.

"You the Brooklyn nigga celebrating the birthday in the other VIP, right?" Black asked.

"That's a fact, cuz. Why what's moving?"

"Nah, it's my birthday too."

"Oh ok y'all in the other VIP? Happy C-Day," NH said going to take a piss.

"Same to you, bro. <y cousin Stacks be in Brooklyn heavy," Black said with a slurred speech because he was tipsy. NH's mind paused thinking about Stacks since he was the man Murda was hunting.

"I don't believe I've heard of him. He must be out here a lot," NH said flushing the stall.

"Yeah sometimes he be at my spot in the pjs on 7th, but I'ma get back to the party. Tryna take some of these thots back to my crib. I see a couple new bartenders in this bitch," Black said leaving NH washing his hand as he came up with a plan.

***

The Next Day
Mount Vernon, NY

Murda knew it was time as he climbed out an old Nissan Maxima with tints parked in the back of a large tall project building.

The morning, NH met up with and explained what happened and Murda couldn't believe it. NH followed Black and two chicks to this building. He even followed them into the parking lot where he overheard Black tell one of the chicks, he was too drunk to get to apartment 6A, so she would have to lead the way to his crib.

Black was so drunk, he vomited all over the lobby floor. NH could've killed him, but he understood Murda needed him alive rather than dead.

Murda was dressed in all black with a ski mask as the snow outside made February look like the North Pole. It was close to midnight and the building was empty as he slid upstairs to the sixth floor.

Once on the sixth floor, Murda saw apartment A to his right. He pulled out his tools he used for breaking into homes to enter.

When he was inside, he pulled out his Glock 17 and walked through the dark crib to hear *South Park* playing loud on TV in the living room.

Murda saw a black nigga laying on the living room couch snoring with his hand in his shorts on his dick.

WHACK! Murda pistol slapped him in his face.

"Ahhhh," Black screamed in pain as his face quickly swelled up.

"Where is Stacks?"

"Who? Man, you got the wrong crib," he said as Murda slapped him again with the butt of his gun, almost knocking him out.

"Where is he? I won't ask you again," Murda said cocking his pistol meaning business.

"Ok he's in Brooklyn with some Spanish bitch. She's sexy. I saw her once. She's classy and thick. She looks like a model."

"Name?"

"I believe Elena."

"Did he mention anything about a kid?" Murda said as Black's bloody face looked sad because he knew who the man was now. He overheard Stacks on the phone in the bathroom cursing and yelling at someone about the baby he kidnapped being killed.

"I'm sorry man, I swear I didn't even know."

"Know what? Talk!" Murda said yelling.

"The chick killed the baby and tossed it out the window. I overheard Stacks confirm it on the phone the other day."

Murda was stuck as he was crying because it made sense. There was a big story about someone strangling a baby and tossing it out the window in the Pink Houses, where he was from.

Black was still talking but Murda couldn't hear a word he said. He shot Black seven times in the head, then made his exit, wishing he never came because that was the last thing he wanted to hear.

***

Meanwhile
Upper Westside, NY

"Ohhh yess! Fuck this pussy," Margaret yelled in the hotel room as her legs were spread wide open as NH dick dived in and out her pussy as she went crazy.

As soon as they met in the hotel, they talked, laughed took some Molly and it was on and popping.

Margaret's pussy was warm, extra tight and so wet, he was slipping and sliding in her as the sheets was soaked.

NH slid his big hard dick with force against her thin vaginal lips and swollen pink clit moistening it with her juices, as he went deeper with each stroke. She dug her long-manicured nails into his chiseled back.

"Uhhhhh yesss harder," she screamed as she felt him deeper into her pelvis. She grabbed his ass, pumping him hard into her. "Ugh! Shit I'm cumming," she yelled as he pulled out to see her squirt like a waterfall laying on her back.

NH placed his dick in her mouth while she was still climaxing. Her thick lips circled his dick as he watched her cheeks hollow as she sucked his cock as he filled her mouth up with watery cum.

"Damn a nigga about to cuff you," he said getting dressed with his back turned to her as she let out a laugh.

"That was some good dick. Too bad."

"Never too bad. We can meet tomorrow," NH said turning around to see her fully dressed with a gun aimed on him

"I don't think so," Susanna stated smiling. "I'm Susanna." NH knew the name. She ran one of the Mob families. He was pissed he let some pussy take him out, especially from a white bitch.

"Can I at least get some more head before you kill me?"

"Wish I could trust me, but I have to go," she said shooting him ten times in the chest with her silencer on a 40 cal.

Romell Tukes

Chapter Twenty-Seven

Yonkers, NY
Months later

Murda was waiting in a building he recently bought. He planned to fix it up and turn it into a homeless shelter for the poor.

He hadn't been the same since the news of his son, but the hardest part was telling his wife Jamika. She went crazy, Murda didn't even know who she was anymore.

Jamika quit her job, stayed at home and refused to go anywhere. She hadn't said a word since he broke the news to her. She was yelling and screaming in her sleep. There would be nights where Murda would wake up in the middle of the night to see her up staring at the wall.

Murda tried to touch her pussy one night to see if she still had any sexually emotion, but she just stared at him as if he was crazy are someone she didn't know.

He tried to feed her, but she refused to eat anything besides yogurt. e wanted his wife back. He was hurt too about the loss of his son, but he had to remain strong for his loved ones, especially while they were in a time of war.

Today he was meeting with a woman named Carmilla from the Colombian Cartel, for whatever reason. He informed her that he would only do one on one's, no guards and she agreed.

Murda knew who the woman was, and he cared nothing for her at all. His pops told him everything about her and about how much of a snake she was.

Web also told him how much he did love her and how she was still his wife. Murda saw the text from Carmilla saying she was outside. When he looked out his window, he saw her getting out a yellow cab.

The apartment was half empty besides furniture, a bar, kitchen, and rugs. There were eight floors with ten apartments on each floor and a basement that looked like a ballroom full of pit bulls.

Murda let Carmilla in. When he laid eyes on her perfect body sitting luscious in her Coach dress and her sexy face, he knew why his father was in love with her.

"Hey Murda," she said looking at him and how sexy he was with his high yellow complexion curly hair, green eyes and muscle build.

"I have to pat you down," he said as she agreed and he did a quick pat down, feeling her soft thick curves and smelling her Prada and Coach perfume. He then opened her purse to pull out a big 50 cal fully loaded.

"A girl gotta protect herself," she said, sitting down smiling as he placed her gun in his lower back.

"How can I help you?"

"Do you mind if I have a drink?" She said crossing her nicely shaped legs.

"Sure, I'll have one too," Murda said getting up to make two drinks.

"I've heard a lot about you Murda. I'm sure we both know how were connected."

"You mean *was* connected! My father is dead."

"Your father can never be dead in spirit," she said sadly as he brought two drinks on a tray. He sat the tray down and went to close the bar cabinets.

Carmilla poured something inside of one of the drinks she pulled out her pussy in a capsule.

"What happen to the FBI job?" he said walking back into the living room area grabbing the glass of liquor closest to her as her face turned sour because he grabbed the wrong glass.

"I had to move forward," she said as he sat across from her.

"Now you run the Colombian Cartel. You know what my father said you would," Murda said taking a sip of his drink, black Henny.

"I'm sure, but I'm here to speak to you about networking. I know you're not heavy in the game, but your name is like God out here. I want to take open shop in Brooklyn. I already have some sections of the Bronx, but Brooklyn is a goldmine." she said.

"I'm out the game, Carmilla"

"I know but it's a kid name Gunna I need removed or some-one to speak to him. He almost killed me months ago, but I'm willing to let bygones be bygones for turfs," she said.

"I believe I heard of him, but my life is focused on other things these days, so I'm not trying to get in the middle of the chaos," he said drinking his Henny.

"I understand."

"Good. Drink please," Murda said looking at her.

"I'm ok, It's a little early. I didn't realize what time it was," she said with a fake smile.

"No please, I insist, drink." he said seriously.

"I'm not feeling well. I'ma call me cab," she said pulling out her phone.

"Bitch!! I said drink," Murda said pointing her own gun at her as she knew she fucked up.

"Ok calm down" she said picking up the glass gulping it down. "Happy?" she said.

"Yeap. Now how's business in Colombia?" Murda said as Carmilla's eyes got low and she started to talk slow dragging her words as Murda smiled. Less than two minutes later, Carmilla was passed out.

***

Twenty Minutes Later

Carmilla woke up in a basement chained to the wall and her ankles were too, as she was bent over on all fours with her body humped over a metal box.

She looked around to see the biggest pit bulls she ever seen surrounding her chained to the walls barking and growling.

Carmilla couldn't move due to the angle she was in, but she felt wind brushing hard against her ass and pussy as her dress was lifted and thongs were cut off exposing her pretty, large pussy.

"Why Carmilla? That's all I want to know," Murda asked coming from around the corner.

"Murda please don't do this. I wasn't going to kill you," she begged.

"Oh, so you were just going to do what? Rape me? Suck me off? Shit you could have asked me to do that, love and not to mention, I would have loved to," he said staring at her phat pussy standing next to her.

"So, what's stopping you?" she said sexually, hoping she was only chained up so he could fuck her.

"There is a lot stopping me but I'm sure my dogs wouldn't mind," he said as he grabbed one of the pits unchaining him.

The big red nose pit went up to Carmilla's ass sniff and within seconds, the dog jumped on her back and pumped his hard dick into her pussy fucking her.

"Uhmm nooo. Murda please," Carmilla cried out as the dog was fucking the shit out of her.

Murda was laughing as he watched his dog, Drama's face once he nutted in her. Murda unleashed a blue noise pit as he raced to Carmilla and fucked her hard. "Ugh stop. I'm sorry," Carmilla yelled as the dog clawed her back and dress badly, as the blue nose growled as he pumped in and out roughly holding on to her big thick ass for support.

All four dogs were in heat, so they was all horny and thirsty as he gave him all a chance to fuck before locking them up.

"Here go your phone. Never try to cross me. The only reason you're not dead is because my father," he said placing her phone next to her fingers so she can call for help as she was in pain and embarrassed, as her ass was scratched badly and pussy filled with cum.

Chapter Twenty-Eight

Cortland, NY

Jamika was in the basement section of their new 14,871 square foot mansion built from cobblestone in the late eighteenth century. The palace had six rooms, two master suites, a guest house, a private vineyard, a six-car garage, a thirty-five-foot gate entrance, and it was a smart house.

Jamika hadn't taken a shower in days since Murda had to hand wash her. She sat on the couch reading the newspaper clip of the baby being thrown out the window last year in the winter.

Tears formed her dark eyes as she didn't even know who she was anymore. She felt lost and out of place.

She overheard Murda tell someone who came to see him that Elena killed his son, and they must find her. Jamika knew the name because the woman was on the FBI's top ten list for years, but her country would never turn her over to them because she had them all on a payroll.

Jamika came up with a plan as she did her research on Elena and today, she is putting her plan into motion. She was dressed in all black with black pain on her face.

***

Rye, NY

Elena just got out the shower from a long day of dealing with Stacks and his worries. She had to call home for some more goons to arrive because she been losing a lot of soldiers.

Murda was still out there and she was doing everything to find him because she was losing sleep every night.

She wore nothing under her Gucci rope as she locked her master bedroom door and walked over to her private make-up area.

Elena placed cream on her face, which was for anti-aging. She took care of herself at all costs, that's why so looked so sexy.

After killing Murda's child, things went bad with her and Stacks because he was using the baby as leverage and she was only there for revenge.

Once she cleaned off her face, she laid down, turning off her lamp light as the outside light from her terrace gave the room a little light.

Within seconds of getting comfortable, she thought she heard a noise as she looked out her bedroom balcony unaware of the shadow lurking behind her.

Jamika grabbed her neck and choked her, pushing her body into her waterbed with powerful force, strangling her throat as Elena tried to fight back, but the crazy woman was too strong.

Her oxygen supply was cut off, making Elena pass out, as Jamika mumbled something before, she pulled out a ten-inch knife.

She circled her knife around her heart, then she stabbed her heart with so much force, the knife almost went out of Elena upper back.

It took Jamika less than ten minutes to carve her heart out, before leaving through the front door, the same way she entered earlier when Elena was out. She was hidden in her closet.

Elena's goons were all in the guest house sleep, so Jamika had an easy get away as she had an awkward smile on her face walking down the street to her Lexus coupe Murda recently brought her.

Jamika had the bloody heart in her cargo pant pocket.

***

Fairfield, CT

Michael and his best friend Franky rode through town in Michael's white Acura NSX.

Michael was eighteen years old on his way to an Ivy League college in Washington. His father was a rich businessman and his mother lived in New York, but he rarely saw her.

His father raised him because his mom Susanna had a busy life in New York.

"Bro I thought you said your mom was coming out here again," Franky asked in the passenger seat listen to a Maroon 5 album.

"Why you always asking about my mom, you dick?"

"Because your mom is hot bro."

"Not as hot as your sister and her head game made me…"

"Don't push it Michael. You always throw that shit in my face," Franky said as they stopped at a red light.

Michael was a tall, pretty, white boy with long hair, blue eyes, and swag. All the women loved him including his best friend's sister.

"Why are we just riding around? Let's call them chicks we met at the mall yesterday." Frank said.

"Bro did you see the bottom of them bitches' feet in their sandals.?"

"Oh my God Michael! Look in the gas station," Frank said as Michael saw two bad ass bitches pumping gas into a Ferrari i812 superfast.

"Damn I need some gas anyway," Michael said pulling into the gas station near the Spanish woman in a tank top and short low cut jeans and a cute blonde in a mesh dress with a bikini under as if they were about to go swimming.

Michael and Franky made their way right to the women.

"Excuse us but it's a hot day and y'all look like y'all trying get into some trouble," Franky said as both women look at how short he was, laughing.

"We're on our way to the beach," the blonde said.

"Yeah were going for a swim," the Spanish chick said.

"Well I have a big pool in my backyard. I would love for you both to come. We have drinks and weed there," Michael stated as both women looked at each other.

"Ok we will follow y'all," the Spanish women said as both men eyed both women with hard-ons.

"Let's go," Michael said, grabbing Franky, ready to party with two bad ass bitches.

The two boys cheered and boasted about who was going to fuck which bitch first and which one would be a better fuck.

Once at Michael's house, the place was built for royalty with a red ceramic barrel tile roof, a heated cobblestone driveway, French double front doors, eleven rooms, eight bathrooms, a guest section, marble slab floors, a spacious gym, a whimsical pool deck maze and six land of acres.

"This is a nice house," one of the women said.

"My bed is even better," Michael stated.

"I don't think your bed is big enough for me to fuck you on," the blonde said walking out the back door to the pool area.

The women admired one another's bodies as they hopped into the pool.

"Bro do you see the pussy on the Spanish bitch?" Franky said as they undressed near the bathhouse.

"The blonde got a nice set of racks on her," Michael said as they made their way over to the pool.

"Y'all ready to go for a swim?" the Spanish chick said looking at the teens hard-on and frail bodies.

"You both should do some pushups," the blonde said, smiling as they all hopped in the pool.

"I just started working out, but I bet I can lift you," Franky stated as he lifted the petite Spanish woman in the air as if he was ready to fuck.

"Let me grab some condoms," the Spanish woman said as she climbed out the pool dripping wet to grab her purse.

Michael was so busy talking to the blonde as he grinded on her phat ass with his small dick. When the Spanish woman came back, she placed her gun to Franky's head and blew his brains out into the pool.

Michael started to cry as Gabby climbed out the pool as Zaby had her gun trained at his head.

"I'm sure Susanna would love this," Zaby said shooting Michael in his head as the pool was dark red.

"You want to go for a swim?" Gabby asked getting dressed.

"Maybe another day," Zaby replied looking at two dead bodies float in the red pool.

Romell Tukes

Chapter Twenty-Nine

Milan, Italy

Chelsea and her crew were in her private jet. Since she owned it, she could do as she pleased. The jet was large with fourteen brown leather seats, a dinner table, a bedroom, a bathroom and shower, a kitchen with a personal chef, a fully loaded bar, and flat screen TVs connected to laptops with free Wi-Fi.

She was on her way to the Balenciaga fashion show in Milan tonight and tomorrow was the Celine' fashion show.

Chelsea was a fashion freak. She loved to order her clothes straight from the designers themselves.

Since she was in Italy, she called a meeting with some of the top families, even though they didn't like her for what she done to Donvito. He was a honorable leader and he did a lot for all the other families unlike Chelsea.

Her flight just landed, and she checked her Rolex to see she had an hour before the show started so she planned to eat dinner at a popular restaurant in downtown Milan where the tourist normally visited.

***

Milan, Italy

Murda and Gunna were both getting dressed in Balenciaga suits in the exquisitely designed estate they rented out for the weekend to attend fashion week.

The La Perria was the finest estate in the city placed on four acres, offering panoramic views, 7,297 square feet of single-level living, seventeen foot walls and forty feet ceiling height, retractable sliding doors, resort style pool, spa, cascading waterfall, and three bedrooms, two private bathrooms.

"You look like money," Murda told Gunna walking into his room to see him in a gray two-piece suit with a Balenciaga tie. Murda had on the same outfit but in black.

"Good looking bro. I love it out here. That club we went to last night was popping. We gotta come back out here one day son," Gunna said placing two pistols in his hostlers.

"No question. We needed this especially with everything going on," Murda stated.

"Facts, you think Jamika will ever be the same?"

"I hope so bro. She hasn't said a word since our son passed, but I got doctors and guards looking after her. I got the camera system on my phone and I've been watching her sit in the same spot all day. Look at this," Murda said pulling out his smart phone showing him a live video of Jamika sitting in the chair in their bedroom playing with her fingers rocking back and forth smiling.

"Damn bro but at least she finally smiling," Gunna said looking at the bright side.

"Yeah I didn't even realize that."

"Bro I couldn't even go to NH's funeral. I'm still hurt about that, but I heard he met with a white bitch at the club so I showed Boogie C a picture of Susanna and he confirmed it was same bitch he saw at the club."

"Damn NH supposed to be more on point, especially dealing with these crackers," Murda said upset because NH was an official nigga.

"When we get back, we going to handle it. Can you believe Zaby and Gabby took out Silvio? I don't even know how them two met," Gunna said laughing.

"That's a crazy match up. Them two together is dangerous bro. If you think about it, the women are putting more work than us" Murda said seriously.

"Damn that's a fact."

"It's time. You ready?" Murda said checking his all black Richard Miller watch worth $4.2 Million.

"Why ask? " Gunna said with a smirk.

"Good stick to the plan. Be in and out, then we enjoy the show, Blood," Murda stated as they both left with one mission on their mind.

***

An Hour Later

The Balenciaga fashion show was packed with guest from all over the world. From the rich to the poor. Models walked up and down the runway in catwalks, sporting all the latest Balenciaga gear.

Chelsea and her guards had front row seat watching the show knowing their boss was leaving with a truck load fill of Balenciaga gear.

She wore red devil satin and crepe Balenciaga two piece showing her stomach, legs, and titties poking out attracting a lot of attention.

While watching the show, she saw two men walk in on the other side taking seats in the front row. Chelsea looked hard and when she saw it was Murda, her heart almost jumped out her skin.

She was ready to kill them right now, but the place had police, the news, and thousands of witnesses so she told her main guard on the right of her that after the show the two men across the runway were dead.

She wondered where their guards were. She didn't even see them look her way. She wondered if they knew she was even here.

All types of thoughts ran through her mind. A waitress walked past her with glasses of champagne. She grabbed both glasses and downed them knowing it was going to be a long night in Milan.

Chelsea looked over at Murda and Gunna who both raised their glasses to her smiling as she got pissed raising her middle finger.

Within seconds, Chelsea body overheated as her oxygen started to cut off. Chelsea started to vomit everywhere. Her guards tried to call for help and do CPR as her body went into shock.

Everybody was so focused on Chelsea, they forgot about the show, as Chelsea died before help could even arrive.

Murda and Gunna slid out the back as Ariana was waiting in an Apollo Intenza Emozione sedan worth $1.7 million with butterfly doors.

"I did good," Ariana said in her waitress uniform.

"You did great," Murda said as him and Gunna hoped in the foreign car pulling off. Mission complete.

***

Brooklyn, NY

Gabby was in a local cheap hotel room on her laptop looking at photos of her and Tookie from years ago when they went to Jamaica and had the time of their life. That was the first time she ever pet a tiger and lion. She was scared to death that day.

With her daughter and lover dead, she felt alone in this world. She felt as if she didn't belong here, but she had to remain strong for herself.

Killing became her medicine for her lately, but she knew she couldn't do it forever, but she planned to enjoy it while it lasted.

Gabby just received an email video clip from Murda it popped up on her laptop as mail. She sat up on the bed in her sweat suit with an awkward look on her face.

She put on her glasses and pushed play on the video to see it was from Milan it was a news clip.

"Good evening this is Ms. Vittomo reporting live from the Momelil de Halani fashion show where a very powerful, dangerous, mobster who is known as the "Godmother", the daughter of the legendary Donvito Da Don, was believed to poisoned here today, which was the same cause of her father's death. Chelsea was dead before help could arrive. Reporting living from Milan," the reporter said from outside of a large brick building where people were leaving out of.

Gabby closed her laptop with tears she grabbed her phone and texted Murda, "Thank you."

She was so happy. The bitch who ruined her life was dead. Karma was a bitch and that was well example.

She had to use the bathroom as she wiped her tears. Gabby was on her period, but her tampons were outside in her Hellcat, so she put on her AirMax 95 shoes matching her Fendi sweat suit.

Gabby went outside into the hotel parking lot, which was low-key and quiet as she liked. She knew nobody would find her here. She got inside her car and grabbed a small bag from the backseat as soon as she turned around an assault rifle was placed to her skull.

"Freeze! FBI!" an officer said before he snatched her out the car and tossed her on the floor as agents and local police came from everywhere. Red and Blue lights flooded the lot as they placed the cuffs on her. Gabby didn't show a lick of emotion as they placed her in a caged SUV.

Chapter Thirty

Cortland, NY

Murda walked into his mansion back from his successful trip.

"What's popping with y'all?" Murda told his friends and goons in the living room as he saw niggas outside shooting dice around and ready for whatever.

"Glad you back, yo. Let me holler at you in the kitchen," Big Hill told his boss leading him into the private kitchen area.

"What's up Hill?" Murda said grabbing two bottles of water for him and Jamika.

"The doctor just left again but he said he'll be back later."

"Ok that's good," Murda said about to walk off until Big Hill stopped him.

"Murda, he said Jamika needs real help. He says she's in a bad connection, man."

"Let me be in charge of that decision."

"Look man nobody wants to hear their loved one is in a bad place mentally. That's how I lost my daughter," Big Hill said looking into Murda's colorful eyes before he walked off without saying a word.

Murda went upstairs in the room to see Jamika sitting in the same chair, in the same clothes, doing the same thing she was before he left.

When Jamika saw him, her pretty eyes widen as he just stood there thinking what Big Hill said. His his daughter died of a mental illness at an early age because he didn't get her any help.

Murda smelled a strong odor in the room he knew he would have to bathe her, so he made his way into their master bathroom to run her warm bubble bath.

Truth was, he hated to see her like that. It brought tears to his eyes because he felt as if it was all his fault and karma for all he done.

"Jamika time for a bath honey," Murda said as he walked out the bathroom to see her standing right there almost scaring him in her gown with a photo and a piece of red meat in her hand with strings attach to it.

When Murda got close, he saw it wasn't red meat, it was a heart.

"How did you get that?" he said snatching the heart and photo out her hand as she ran back to her chair playing with her fingers rocking back and forth.

Murda saw it was a photo of Elena from his file he kept of all his enemies and she was the top of the list after killing their child.

"You killed her?" Murda asked softly as she nodded her head up and down non-stop. He was at a loss of words. *But how* he thought to himself and why would she cut out her heart?

Murda called Big Hill upstairs and gave him the heart and told him what happen, he was shocked.

"I saw that shit on the news the other day that a Rye woman was strangled to death and her fucking heart was cut out, but they never said no names. I don't even know how she left the house," he stated holding the heart feeling sick.

"Don't worry about it. Just get rid of that," he said walking back into the room to see her still nodding her head up and down, playing with her fingers.

Murda had tears in his eyes as he just watched from a distant as she acted as if he wasn't even there.

He bathed her and fed her, then put her to sleep as he made an important call to the mental health doctor, requesting the best mental health hospital in the state.

***

Utica, NY

Murda and Jamika rode in the back of a 650 white Maybach this morning on their way to the best treatment center in New York to get Jamika help.

Big Hill pulled in front of the estate that looked like a college with pools, a tennis court, a golf course, basketball court, mountain views, and the strong smell of fresh air.

Murda led Jamika out the car as Big Hill grabbed the bags out of the trunk, and they walked up the stairs of the main building.

Inside was clean, full of patients and staff walking around catering to the clients. Murda made his way to the front desk to see an older black woman doing paperwork of some sort.

"Excuse, I'm Jamel and this is Jamika."

"Oh yes we been waiting on you. Wow she is beautiful," the older woman said looking at Jamika's long hair in a ponytail, her Chanel suit and heels and manicured nails. Murda made sure she had her hair and nails done because regardless, she was still a bad bitch and his queen.

"Thanks," Murda said holding her hand as she squeezed it tightly.

"Follow me. I'ma lead you to her room. This is the lobby area and dayroom where they would come to play table games, take meds, and to watch whatever they like," she said giving him the tour.

Murda saw men and women talking and yelling to themselves. He saw one man licking the floor as a nurse rushed to his aid to stop him then he saw a young cute white woman swimming on the floor in a corner yelling about sharks.

"Don't mind the crazy shit. This is regular until it's time for their meds. We have the best mental health doctors in the state. Most of our clients were able to get better and leave to live a regular life, but some can't get right," the older black lady said walking down the hallway that looked like a dorm.

"Who will be her doctor?" Murda asked.

"Ms. Green. She is our best, trust me and this is her room," she said entering the large room with two flat screen TVs, a big glass window overlooking the backyard and mountain tops, two leather chairs, a big bed, a private bathroom, a walk-in closet, a dresser and big mirror on the wall.

"When can I visit?"

"Weekends and holidays."

"You like this baby?" he asked Jamika who just sat on her new bed liking how soft it was as she bounced up and down like a kid as Big Hill brought four duffle bags into her walk- in closet.

"Nice," Big Hill said surprised at how nice the room was. Murda pulled out a wad of blue faces and handed it to the lady

"No please, I love helping and she reminds me so much of my daughter, but no worries. She will be well taken care of. I'll give you my personal number to update you."

"That will be great, thank you." Murda said hoping this was all Jamika needed to come back to life.

"Sure."

"Ok, Jamika were leaving," Murda said loudly kissing his wife on her forehead as she just stared at the window to see people outside.

Murda left feeling a half of him just left his soul as he pulled away from the estate.

***

Lower Eastside, NY

Susanna was in the back of her new Bentley Bentayga SUV as her driver followed the SUV in front of them with her soldier leading the way through the dark New York streets.

A couple of weeks ago, she had to put her son in the ground that was worse than burying her father recently.

She felt as if death was all around her from Silvio, and the recent shocking news of Chelsea's death.

Susanna didn't have enough manpower to go against Murda because he was a force to be fucked with, so she was moving to Miami. She tried to reach out to Fernando, but it was as if he was a ghost in the wind.

There was one stop she had to make before getting on her private jet. She had five million dollars in her storage unit, which she was on the way to now.

Susanna used her key to get inside the storage warehouse. She made it to garage #17 when she lifted the garage door, a Tech9 sub machine gun was pointed at her head.

"Looking for me bitch," Ariana said.

"I don't even know you but do what you have to do. Y'all niggers and spicks, or whatever you are, already took everything I love so you're doing me the favor," Susanna said sitting there in her black dress and heels as Ariana wore her Army uniform. "What happened to women empowerment?" Susanna said making Ariana laugh as she had to laugh herself before Ariana shot her six times.

Susanna's guards ran inside, only to meet her bullets, killing them all. Ariana walked out smoothly. She already disconnected the cameras and the alarm. Ariana hopped in her Lexus texting Gunna a smiley face, which was there code for job done, successfully.

Romell Tukes

Chapter Thirty-One

F.B.I. Headquarters

Gabby had been in the Federal building for days, in and out of bullpens and interrogation rooms as police threatened her and tried to get her to spill some beans.

When she heard what she was being charged with, chills went up her body, but she knew this day could come. She was being charged with the murder of Officer Edmond close to five years ago in a movie theater parking lot.

Gabby thought she would be arrested for one of her recent murders, but that wasn't the case at all. She still wondered why they would wait years later to arrest her. It didn't make sense to her, but she was happy all of her assault rifles, pistol, and grenades were all next door in a different hotel room under a fake name.

"You ready to talk bitch?" an older white man said walking into the cold room in his suit that smelled like cigar smoke.

Gabby never saw this cop before, but they would rotate daily as if that was going to break her, but it only made her laugh and shake her head.

"I'm Lieutenant Edmond Sr., the leading officer of your case. Do you know why I took this case when my boss brought it to my attention, before he was murdered in his garage, which I hope you had something to do with," he said sitting across from her.

"No, please tell me. I'm sure you will anyway," she said smartly.

"Officer Edmond was my son. My only boy," the lieutenant stated.

"Sorry to hear that. I guess life isn't fair for nobody. Guess that's how life goes," she said as the lieutenant reached over the table and slapped the shit out of her.

"You watch your fucking mouth little bitch."

"That's how you hit a woman? My grandma hits harder than that, you dick," she said laughing as the side of her face swelled up.

"Keep that same energy when you get a life sentence," he said leaving pissed off.

Twenty minutes later, another man walked in with food and a briefcase.

"You can keep your food, you fucking pig."

"You must be Gabby. Your cousin told me you were rough around the edges. I'm Mr. Britton, your lawyer," he said as Gabby now sat up because he got her attention. She took the deli sandwich and soda looking at his Michael Kors suit and clean cut.

"Who hired you?" Gabby asked crushing her turkey and cheese sandwich that tasted like Arby's.

"Phoebe," he said as she smiled because her cousin always came through in hard times.

"Ok so what going on?" she said.

"This case is crazy because it's a lot of things that aren't adding up. It's like they want you for something else, but they're pinning the cop murder on you to break you. Mr. Cavallori is the one who re-opened the cop case," the lawyer said flipping through papers.

"Hold on Mr. Cavallori? Does he have a daughter?"

"Yes, he does. She was recently found dead. Do you know them?" he asked.

"No, I just know of the Cavallori Hair Salon downtown."

"Oh ok, but this was a cold case. You must of pissed someone off real bad or someone is out to get you because this case is bullshit, but it's enough to get a conviction. I'ma do my best to help. It's my job plus the $500k I was paid. My name depends on it and this is a big case. I'ma do some research and come visit you. I believe they are taking you to MDC Brooklyn a hold over, so just sit tight. It may take months or even years to get a trial date," her lawyer said before leaving her with a little hope.

***

Brooklyn, NY
Weeks later

Murda had been going to church alone, lately, finding himself getting closer with the man upstairs. Things were quiet since most of the Mobsters was dead besides Fernando who was in hiding, but Gunna was on his heels.

He went to visit Jamika every weekend and she wasn't getting no better. The only word she said was Murda and when people heard her say this all day, they stayed far away from her.

With everything that was going on, he'd forgotten he had a life. He planned to visit YB and Tookie's gravesite sometime this week, but today was a bad day because it was a bad snow storm in New York and snow was up to eight inches.

Hearing about Gabby's arrest made him feel sad for her because she was a ride or die chick and she was family. Zaby went to see her weekly in MDC Brooklyn because they were close. He was confused as to how it happened, but it did.

Murda walked out the church in his Hermes hoodie bubble coat with a scurf, unable to see through the thick clouds of snow fogging up the city streets.

Once he made it to his black Porsche Cayenne Turbo truck, he climbed in and turned on the heat rubbing his hands together trying to warm up because it was below ten degrees outside.

He wondered how he was going to make it home in this storm. He chose to stay at Gunna's condo across town blocks away.

As soon as he pushed the push to start button under the steering wheel, he heard a tap on his window making him look.

Boc!

Boc!

Boc!

Boc!

The gunman ran off after shooting Murda in the head, leaving him slumped in his Porsche.

A man came out of nowhere, shooting at the gunman who got shot in the leg, as the man continued to try to gun him down. The gunman was able to get away as the Spanish man opened the Porsche door and placed Murda's body in the passenger seat, rushing him to the hospital he saw to block down on his way to the church.

Chapter Thirty-Two

Augusta, Maine

Fernando and his girlfriend Dakota just arrived at the ski slopes in the mountains just minutes away from their home.

Today was snowy as regular this was an area where tourist would come to snowboard, ride snowmobiles, and ski on the deep slopes.

It had been over a year since Fernando been back to New York around all the mayhem and he was glad because he was now the last man standing.

When he heard about Chelsea's death in the Mafia motherland, he knew Murda was responsible and he gained a load of respect for him. He was still able to run his businesses from a distance in New Jersey to keep steady income because Dakota was expensive.

"Let's do the snowmobiles today baby," Dakota said as she was bundled up in North Face gear to stay warm because it was freezing.

"Are you sure? It's a little icy baby," Fernando stated as they walked into a snowmobile shop

"We'll be ok. Stop being so scared. You must try new things. We've been cooped up in the house for months. Let's live freely," Dakota said in her hippie voice as Fernando tagged along.

They paid to rent the two-blue fast snowmobiles out and brought some helmets for safety cautious.

The couple drove through the mountain slopes with other snowmobiles speeding around corners over deep mountain cliffs as if they were pros.

Fernando slowed down because Dakota was going too fast. When she looked back, he stopped making her stop and make a U-turn.

"What's wrong baby?" Dakota asked him as he took off his helmet with his frozen lips and ears.

"Let's go back. We're too far out," he said looking around to see only snowy mountains above them.

"I know you're not scared," she said laughing as a red snowmobile raced around the corner with a black guy in a helmet and Gucci snow outfit.

Dakota had a thing for black dudes. She tried to see his face, but the visor on his helmet was dark, but she could see his hand and neck.

This was the first snowmobile they saw this far out. He must be lost or sightseeing as most tourist did every day to take pictures.

When Fernando saw the man stop, he felt a funny that something wasn't right.

Tat!
Tat!
Tat!
Tat!
Tat!
Tat!
Tat!
Tat!

The man lifted a Mack 10, firing shots into Fernando's head, as his body flipped off the snowmobile.

Dakota tried to race off until shots entered her lower back as her snowmobile swerved off the cliff and her body fell into the 297 ft mountain cave.

Gunna raced back up the hill the same way he came, laughing because the look on Fernando's face was the look on a niggas mug shot when he was ready to tell on a bunch of niggas.

He been watching Fernando all day since he came into the town to go snowmobiling. It just so happened he saw him at a nearby diner eating breakfast with Dakota across the street from his hotel.

Gunna kidnapped Fernando's manager at one of his pizza shops and tortured him until he gave up Fernando's location, which was to easy.

With Murda in the hospital in a coma, Gunna was knocking off anybody until he found his brother's shooter. He was happy his brother made it because the doctor told Gunna most people shot in the spot Murda got hit, didn't make it.

The doctor also informed him it was a forty to sixty percent chance of him making it out the coma. The doctor informed him that if it wasn't for the Spanish young man that brought him in the hospital at the time he did, then he would be dead.

Gunna drove the snowmobile back to the tourist main area and left it as he planned to hop on a flight back to New York in two hours.

***

Utica, NY

Jamika had been staring at the TV for four days now since the news played a report about a businessman being gunned down in a snowstorm outside of a church in Brooklyn.

When she saw Murda's face, she cried especially when the news reporter said it didn't look like the victim was going to make it.

She stayed in her room all day. She never left. Her food and meds were brought to her at certain hours of the day.

Her doctor put her on five different types of crazy meds, which had her gaining weight, unable to sleep, breaking out in rashes on her skin, and made her shake uncontrollably.

"It's time for your meds, you little bitch," the older black woman who gave her and Murda the tour guide when she first came, said.

Jamika shook her face no for the meds as the woman grabbed her frail face with her big old hands and forced the meds down her throat.

"I brought your dinner too," the older lady said smiling as she grabbed a tray of carrots, rice, cooked beef, and jell-o off the dresser.

The woman placed the tray of food in front Jamika on a cart in front of her bed. She looked at Jamika's crazy wild hair smiling.

"Oh, before I forget, my special seasoning," she said hog spitting in Jamika's food before walking out laughing.

Jamika didn't touch the food as she continued to rock back and forth saying the name Murda repeatedly. She pulled out a sharp razor blade from under her pillow as she stopped rocking and traced the razor on her forearm veins.

"Sor-r-r-r-y Murda. I'm late I'm coming with you baby," Jamika said with tears as she slit her left wrist so deep, her blood vessels were hanging out as blood poured everywhere like a spring fountain.

Jamika's pulse stopped as she died in her bed with a smile on her face. She bled for close to an hour, leaving her bed soaked.

The staff did rounds every hour to check on the patients. When the staff member saw Jamika laying in a pool of blood and not responding, he called the nurses.

Jamika was already long gone before the EMS and police arrived called the forensic scientistand examiners to investigate the crime scene. Ultimately, they classify it as a suicide.

The old black lady who served Jamika her food and meds had on a fake sad face, but deep down so was happy.

Years ago, Jamika arrested her son Tank from Newburg on a gang indictment and she got her only son one hundred years in feds plus a life sentence in state prison.

Her son ended up hanging himself in his cell in Florence USP in Colorado, so this was music to her dirty ears.

Chapter Thirty-Three

Brooklyn, Hospital

Ariana hopped out her all white new Audi S5 coupe with peanut butter seats and pitch-black tints. She wore an off-white business suit with high heels, looking like a sexy businesswoman, as she made her way into the hospital where her brother was.

Since hearing about what happened to him, she been in a depressed faze because everything she cared for was slowly being snatched from her.

She thought after killing Chelsea, things would go back to normal, but from the looks of it shit was getting worse.

"Excuse me I'm here for a Jamel."

"Jamal what?" the lobby clerk stated rudely while on the phone talking to her baby daddy arguing over child support payments he missed.

"Jamel Taylor," she replied not trying to go back and forth with the bitch.

"The rich sexy dude in the coma? He in room 207 on the fourth floor the ICU unit," the fat ugly clerk stated popping her bubble gum, ice grilling Ariana.

"Thank you," Ariana said making her way to the elevator as nurses and doctors conversed about the life, they saved minutes ago.

Ariana was in the elevator texting an old friend smiling to herself as she got off on her floor with a couple of nurses.

She walked down the bright, clean, shiny hall to inhale the smell of death. This was one reason why she hated coming to hospitals.

Once at room #207, she saw her brother in a hospital bed plugged up to IV machines with a headwrap bandage around his head. She saw he was sleep in a coma. She felt so sad for him, but she knew this came with the street life.

Ariana walked in the cold room and pulled a chair next to his bed.

"Hey brother I'm sorry about what happened and sorry for taking so long to pull up, but I hate hospitals. I smell death. I can't believe what happened. Gunna is going crazy or brazy with a capital B, as you say," she chuckled. "He wants to kill the whole town, but I tell him it's ways you supposed to handle things like this and killing everybody isn't the way. We'll all be in jail or dead at the blink of an eye. Facts, but I wish we could have met when we were kids or younger because a lot would've been different. A lot, trust because this isn't the type of life I wanted as a little girl. I wanted to be a teacher for kids with special needs, but instead I went to the Navy and went through so much as a person wouldn't believe because they see a pretty face, but it's a lot of pain and hurt under these eyes," she said trying hold back her tears, listening to the machines beep.

"I'm praying you one day wake up, but what I'm about to tell you, is going make you wish you stayed in this coma away from pain, hurt, and grief. Your wife recently killed herself. She slit her wrist. Me and Gunna just found out. I'm sorry Murda. I know it's the worse feeling. I must go. I hope you get well soon but I have something to tell you. I'm not who you think I am. There is a lot about me you don't know, but unfortunately you will soon take care," she said kissing his hand laying on the bed before she turned to leave.

"Excuse me, but you can't be here. It's no visitors in this area at this time," a young white nurse said looking at her.

"Ok I was just leaving. How is he doing?" Ariana asked on her way out.

"Not good. He's in a coma."

"Of course," Ariana said walking down the hall shaking her head.

***

Utica, NY

Stacks was on his way to get his girl back. He found out Jamika was in a mental rehab upstate in Utica and he was on his way to get her out, even if he had to go out gun blazing.

Stacks saw want happened to Murda on the news and he was happy, but he wished he was the one who could of took him out of his misery, but someone beat him to the punch.

Now with his main problems solved, he could force on rebuilding a relationship with Jamika, even if she was mentally ill. He could help groom her into her old self.

He was driving through long country roads full of acres of land, farms, animals and riverbanks. Stacks heard what happened to Elena and his heart went out to her since hers was cut out. He never knew Murda was that sick to cut a bitch's heart out.

Stacks seen a rehab center sign ahead, the same one Jamika was at. She was ten miles away. He pulled off the exit and drove through the small redneck city.

Minutes later, Stacks pulled into the rehab lot to see a nice resort like building with staff going in and out as the shifts were changing.

Stacks walked in the building in his Armani suit, smelling like Gucci Guilty cologne for men with a dozen of French roses in his hand.

"Excuse me. Is a Jamika here?" Stacks asked an older black woman, sitting at the lobby desk reading a Ebony magazine, minding her business.

"Who are you?" she said looking the brother up and down.

"I'm a friend. Is she here are not?"

"You must not watch the news, or you must be a distant friend, because she killed herself weeks ago. The crazy bitch slit her wrist. We don't know the reason, but your princess is dead," the lady stated coldly as she went back to reading her magazine.

"We must have the wrong person," Stacks said nervously pulling out a photo of him and Jamika handing it to her.

She grabbed a newspaper from under her desk with smiley faces drawn all over it in a red pen marker.

Stacks flipped through the paper to see, nothing until he got to page 5A.

Mental Women Slits Her Wrist at Mental Hospital

Stacks read the whole article and even saw a photo of Jamika at the bottom with a mustache drawn on her upper lip.

Stacks said nothing as he grabbed the paper, taking it with him as the old lady laughed like an evil witch. Once in the Ford pickup truck, he started to bang the steering wheel with tears rolling down his face.

He was sick. Jamika was the only thing he had left in life, and now she was gone. He pulled off getting far away from the rehab center as possible.

Realizing he as low on gas, he pulled into a rest stop full of truckers and white racist crackers who looked like they was thirsty to hang and lynch a nigga.

Stacks had to piss as he made his way to the restroom. Inside the dirty restroom, a piss and shit odor filled the room. He went in one of the blue stalls and took a long piss.

"Damn," he said as steam was coming from his piss. Stacks felt cold steel to his head.

"Got you lacking with your pants down. I been following you all day. I knew you would come for Jamika, unaware she dead. Just like a regular tender dick nigga."

Bloc!
Bloc!
Bloc!
Bloc!
Bloc!
Bloc!
Bloc!

Zaby left his dead body in the dirty stall before walking out smiling, climbing in her Hyundai Palisade heading back home to spend time with Gunna.

Chapter Thirty-Four

Zaby was driving on the interstate back to Brooklyn listening to the radio, bopping her head up and down. Gunna was home waiting on her for their dinner date and of course she had big plans for the night cap, which was a long night full blown passionate sex.

She knew Gunna needed comfort right now, especially with Murda in a coma because he wasn't 100% himself without him, so she just wanted to be there the best she could.

Gunna went to Maine to take care of Fernando's scary ass once and for all, while she made it her obligation to handle Stacks, which was a piece of cake.

The only issue was she kinda forgot to tell Gunna she was going to kill him, while she promised him to stay home, but she knew some promises were meant to be broken.

Zaby saw her sister call her digital intel caller on her dashboard connected to her phone.

"Look who is it Mrs. El Chapo herself," Zaby said making her sister laugh.

"Girl you trying to get a bitch indicted. You know that nigga hotter than fish grease," Zainab said.

"Nobody worried about you, but what's up?"

"I'm checking on my sister. Something in my little gut told me to call. I don't know why, but I'm glad you ok."

"Awww that's so sweet."

"Whatever. Where are you anyway? You need to bring your ass home every once in a while," Zainab said really using that excuse because she missed her.

"I'm a married woman now and if you were getting the dick I was getting, this would be your new home too," Zaby said honest making her crack up.

"Bitch you crazy. You know Ramadan starts tonight. Everybody out here is super Muslim now after they been out here paying for pussy, sex trafficking and all types of crazy shit"

"You not no better, "Zaby added.

"I guess you right."

"Hold on sis. This eighteen-wheeler is coming behind me at the speed of light. I hate these New York drivers," Zaby said changing lanes to her right near the woods and trees on the pitch-black highway.

The eighteen-wheeler got on the side of Zaby and with one hard hit, the truck made her car flip twice into a deep ditch. The truck stopped and a gang of men hopped out dressed in all black with machine gun rushing to Zaby.

The impact of the car accident had Zaby dazed, scatterbrained, frivolous and confused, but when the gunmen tossed a conscious military bomb into the ditch, the noise almost made her die as she tried to crawl out with her gun.

The gunmen snatched her up, yelling to each other as she couldn't even move or stand up straight. She was so weak. They threw her into the eighteen wheeler with twenty other men dressed in black before climbing in pulling off.

***

Brooklyn, NY

Gunna was awaiting in his condo for Zaby, dressed in his Prada suit ready to go out for diner, but it was ten at night and Zaby wasn't answering her phone, which was something new because she always answered.

She was supposed to be here. Before he left, he told her to stay put until he got back because he knew how she liked to roam and put in work.

The last text he got from her was earlier when she texted him, she missed him and couldn't wait to suck his dick :).

Gunna stood up to look out his balcony window to hear his phone ring. It was a text from Zainab saying to call her right now

911 emergency, which stopped his heart, but it could only be one thing.

***

Brooklyn Hospital

Murda was still in his coma but tonight he was supposed to be moved downstairs out the ICU unit into a regular unit. The hospital was over filled with cases and the ICU was starting to run out of room, so they were shifting some people around.

Two male doctors in lab coats came into Murda's room to move him and grabbed his bed and IV machines on wheels

They rolled Murda down the hall towards the elevator. When the door opened, they saw two male nurses, one who looked gay and the other one looked as if he hated his job.

"Uhh, you two must be new around here," the white gay nurse said to the two Spanish men transferring Murda. Both men nodded, paying the man no mind as his stop arrived. "Hopefully I'll be seeing you two handsome chunks around more," the gay nurse said strutting his way out the elevator in his tight uniform as the other nurse shook his head getting off on the same floor, wishing he didn't have to.

The doctors got off the at main level as the pushed Murda towards the back exit, as two female nurses were coming inside from a smoke break.

"Excuse me but where are y'all going? This is the lobby, the patient's rooms are upstairs," one of them said as the men continued to push Murda towards the exit.

"Ayyy," the bigger women shouted.

PSST!
PSST!
PSST!
PSST!
PSST!
PSST!
PSST!

One of the men shot one of the women in her head with a pistol with a silencer attached to it as they made the exit to the large van parked feet away.

Once Murda was in safely, they dashed out the lot on the highway to the private jet awaiting them all.

***

Los Santos, Panama
One Month Later

Murda was lying in a large heated comfortable bed hooked to IV's filled with water and meds. He was still in a coma and in a bad condition, but he had five doctors at his side all throughout the day trying to get him better doing tests, new meds, and screenings trying to find a solution.

The room looked like a house itself a private bathroom, private balcony, private bathroom, separate office, high thirty foot ceilings, a library, a sixty-two inch flat screen TV, a spacious view of the seventeen acres of land, heated floors, French made tables, Italian design wallpaper and with open ceilings.

The bedroom double doors opened, and a beautiful Panamanian woman walked in alone in a Celine dress with heels looking no older than nineteen. She was beyond beautiful.

Patricia Herriquez sat next to Murda and held his hand lightly rubbing it hoping he would get better soon, but she had faith because she had the best doctors looking after him.

Patricia was the boss of the Panamanian Cartel, which was one of the deadliest Cartel families known to man and woman. She was thirty-five years old, but looked like a teenager, she was five-four height, orange eyes, and hazel long dark blonde hair, nice C cup breast, Spanish features being as she was 100% Latino, a phat ass with wide curves, no body fat, small waist, thick lips, thick perfect eyebrows, long eyelashes, nice smooth bronze light complexion.

Hands down she was a bad bitch. She was married at the young age of seventeen to Carlos Herriquez, who was the boss of the Panamanian Cartel until he was murdered with her father while she was pregnant with her son Juan, who Carmilla recently killed.

Pat is the one who saved Murda's life the day he was shot. Her capo saved his life and kidnapped him from the hospital to bring him to his boss.

"Jamel I've been watching you for a long time, and I've grown strong emotional feelings for you. One I never even had for my husband. That's not why you're here or why I saved your life. You have some very dangerous people trying to kill you and everything you love. How me and you connect is the same person or people that want you dead, I want them dead. That's why you're here. The people closet to you are the ones against. You won't believe who and why. I'm about the only person you can trust right now, but let me tell you the story from the beginning," she said talking to Murda in his coma as if he was alive telling him the story from the beginning so he would know what they were about to be up against.

Romell Tukes

Chapter Thirty-Five

Brooklyn, NY
One Year Later

It was a hot summer dark night in Brooklyn at Dean street park, which was empty besides Gunna sitting at the wooden alone waiting on his guest of the evening.

Since Zaby was kidnapped, his life hasn't been the same. The police found her car flipped over on a highway near upstate Albany, New York. Her body remains were never found and this is wasn't the worse part. The night she was kidnapped, her sister Zabinab was still on the phone listening to what was going on.

Zainab informed him the men who came to get Zaby were speaking in Arabic language and she could hardly make out what they were saying due to the conscious bomb, but she did her them say something about the U.K.

When Murda was kidnapped from the hospital, he knew there had to be a connection between the crimes and disappearances.

Gunna lost everything he loved slowly, which made him cold-hearted. Business was good as Zainab was still supplying him the best coke and dope in the states, but lately there was a new chief in town by the name of Verman, and he was stepping on his toes. The nigga Verman, opened a couple of shops in Brooklyn, but Gunna crew shut it down before they could even see a hundred grand.

Verman's name was ringing all though cities, from Queens, Staten Island, Long Island and the Bronx from South Bronx to Uptown. Gunna reached out to someone he had a mutual relation-ship in Verman to have a sit down because Gunna was losing money. He was supplying the whole city until Verman.

Gunna came out alone tonight as it was a part of the meeting deal. He saw a now all black McLaren 600LT Spider speed into the lot, looking like a space car with a rear wing on the back.

He saw a woman climb out in an Adidas track suit with heels and a hoodie covering her face. Gunna thought it was a joke as he saw the woman's curves and sexy walk. She strutted up the park gazebo entrance where he was waiting.

When the woman made it up the stairs, Gunna was able to see a little more of her sexy facial features.

"You fucking bitch," Gunna yelled as he pulled out his gun and so did the woman. Now they both had their gun aimed on each other. "Where is my wife?"

"I don't know nothing about no wife. I'm here to talk business, that's all," Carmilla stated pointing her 45 glock handgun at him.

"You Verman?"

"Yeap. I told you I was going to find my way," she said as he got madder.

Carmilla been getting to a big bag lately in his city. She even formed her own crew in the Bronx. She went by the name Verman instead of Carmilla, so people would think she was a man when she is really a bad bitch behind the name.

"Can we talk or we going to shoot it out because I have no time for games. Your men killed a lot of my workers and I lost a lot."

"I should just kill you right now bitch," he said with a grin ready to pull his trigger.

"What's stopping you gangsta?"

"I am," a voice said coming out the shadows as both of them turned around to see the man in an Armani gray suit walking up the stairs

"Murda?" They both said at the same time shocked because they both thought he was dead.

"Put the guns down," he asked as neither one of them listened. "Put it down, please. Nobody is killing nobody here. At least not tonight," he said looking at Carmilla as they both put their guns down.

"Murda how do you know him?" she asked in her Spanish accent.

"He's my brother," Murda said as Carmilla face said it all.

"This is crazy," she stated.

"How do you know this bitch?" Gunna said showing his hate for her.

"Respect Gunna. She was Web's wife before she crossed him, but we got bigger issues. First let deal with Carmilla. I'ma let you have the city except for Brooklyn. My town is off limits," Murda said as Gunna face screwed up.

"What? We have shops in the Bronx and Queens that are doing numbers! Hell nah," Gunna said pacing back and forth.

"That sounds good to me. With that being said, I'll be on my way," she said smiling.

"You got bigger problems to worry about."

"I'm sure I do. Take care and nice to see you. Just to let you know, I never forgot what you did to me."

"I'm sure you didn't," he added with a fake smile.

When she was in her car, Gunna spazzed. "What the fuck you just do bro? I worked hard for them spots," Gunna screamed on him.

"Shut up and listen nigga. We got a bigger problem. I know who got Zaby," he said as Gunna paused and his mind went into overdrive.

"Who?"

"Sit down and listen," Murda said as Gunna did as he was told.

"When I was in a coma I was in a type of coma where I can hear everything a person said, but I just couldn't move, talk, or open my eyes. So, when Ariana come to see me, she said some-things that confused me, but when I got kidnapped, everything came to light bro."

"I knew something was up with Ariana. I ain't see her since you got shot," Gunna stated.

"Ariana isn't who we thought she was bro. She got Zaby, but she wasn't alone. She is married to the head leader of a big terrorist group in Europe and the UK."

"What the fuck?" Gunna said.

"Yeah so the person who kidnapped me told me the whole story while I was in my coma unaware, I could hear, but when I woke up, she told me the story."

"Who and why would she help? Something seems fishy."

"I thought the same thing, but she is the reason why I'm here. The night I was shot, her Capo chased the gunmen down. Come to find out, the shooter was Ariana. Her capo was following her all day. The woman who I speak of is Pat. She runs the Panamanian Cartel and Ariana's husband and her, killed her husband and father years ago. That's why she been on to them and for some reason, we're the terrorist's main targets. They got Zaby somewhere. I believe in the European country," Murda said as Gunna was taking it all in.

"She's in the UK. The night they took her, her sister heard Muslim men speaking Arabic telling each other something about the UK."

"Ok, but this is a big level we're about to enter. These overseas terrorists are different types of gangsta's bro."

"I don't give a fuck about none of that, but if you see Ariana, you won't have any issues killing your sister?" Gunna asked a question he asked himself for weeks.

"She's not family. We're family. You cross the line you stay there."

"Facts, but we should have killed Carmilla."

"Don't worry about her. Pat wants her for herself. Ms. Carmilla got a rude awakening," Murda stated as both men stood to leave.

"You killed Stacks? Pat showed me the news clips of his death at a rest stop."

"No, I wish but that was Zaby's work."

"Wow," Murda said very impressed.

"I gotta meet this Pat."

"Yeah, she's different bro. She helped me heal up. We can trust her bro. Me and her have a clear understanding. Over the months she became special to me. Especially after Jamika's death. When I woke up and found out bro, I was fucked up for months."

Murda said thinking about how hurt he was when he heard Jamika committed suicide.

"Yeah I'm sorry about that," Gunna said knowing that was going to hit him hard.

"Pat helped me get myself back together. I owe her a lot and not to mention, she's a bad bitch in and out."

"How close are the two of you?" Gunna asked as they walked towards the end of the parking lot where a black Rolls Royce Ghost awaited them.

Murda laughed at Gunna's question as he opened the back door to the Rolls Royce to see a beautiful woman step out in a long white Alexander McQueen dress with heels.

"Damn!" was all Guna could say in a loss of words when he saw Pat.

"Hey, Gunna. I'm Pat nice to meet you. I've heard so much about you," she said shaking his hand then kissing Murda on his soft lips. Gunna never saw a bitch so bad and sexy in life. His dick was hard at the sight of her.

"We gotta go you ready," Murda asked Gunna.

"To where?" Gunna asked as Pat and Murda laughed climbing in the Ghost as he followed ready for whatever was ahead.

To Be Continued...

Murda Season 4
Coming Soon

Submission Guideline

Submit the first three chapters of your completed manuscript to ldpsubmissions@gmail.com, subject line: Your book's title. The manuscript must be in a .doc file and sent as an attachment. Document should be in Times New Roman, double spaced and in size 12 font. Also, provide your synopsis and full contact information. If sending multiple submissions, they must each be in a separate email.

Have a story but no way to send it electronically? You can still submit to LDP/Ca$h Presents. Send in the first three chapters, written or typed, of your completed manuscript to:

LDP: Submissions Dept
Po Box 944
Stockbridge, Ga 30281

DO NOT send original manuscript. Must be a duplicate.

Provide your synopsis and a cover letter containing your full contact information.

Thanks for considering LDP and Ca$h Presents.

BOW DOWN TO MY GANGSTA

By **Ca$h**

TORN BETWEEN TWO

By **Coffee**

THE STREETS STAINED MY SOUL **II**

By **Marcellus Allen**

BLOOD OF A BOSS **VI**

SHADOWS OF THE GAME II

By **Askari**

LOYAL TO THE GAME **IV**

By **T.J. & Jelissa**

IF LOVING YOU IS WRONG… **III**

By **Jelissa**

TRUE SAVAGE **VII**

MIDNIGHT CARTEL III

DOPE BOY MAGIC IV

CITY OF KINGZ II

By **Chris Green**

BLAST FOR ME **III**

A SAVAGE DOPEBOY III

CUTTHROAT MAFIA III

By **Ghost**

A HUSTLER'S DECEIT III

KILL ZONE **II**

BAE BELONGS TO ME III

A DOPE BOY'S QUEEN III

By **Aryanna**

COKE KINGS V

Romell Tukes

KING OF THE TRAP II

By **T.J. Edwards**

GORILLAZ IN THE BAY V

3X KRAZY II

De'Kari

THE STREETS ARE CALLING II

Duquie Wilson

KINGPIN KILLAZ IV

STREET KINGS III

PAID IN BLOOD III

CARTEL KILLAZ IV

DOPE GODS III

Hood Rich

SINS OF A HUSTLA II

ASAD

KINGZ OF THE GAME VI

Playa Ray

SLAUGHTER GANG IV

RUTHLESS HEART IV

By Willie Slaughter

THE HEART OF A SAVAGE III

By Jibril Williams

FUK SHYT II

By Blakk Diamond

THE REALEST KILLAZ III

By Tranay Adams

TRAP GOD III

By Troublesome

YAYO IV

GHOST MOB

Stilloan Robinson

KINGPIN DREAMS III

By Paper Boi Rari

CREAM II

By Yolanda Moore

SON OF A DOPE FIEND III

By Renta

FOREVER GANGSTA II

GLOCKS ON SATIN SHEETS III

By Adrian Dulan

LOYALTY AIN'T PROMISED III

By Keith Williams

THE PRICE YOU PAY FOR LOVE II

By Destiny Skai

CONFESSIONS OF A GANGSTA III

By Nicholas Lock

I'M NOTHING WITHOUT HIS LOVE II

SINS OF A THUG II

By Monet Dragun

LIFE OF A SAVAGE IV

A GANGSTA'S QUR'AN III

MURDA SEASON IV

GANGLAND CARTEL III

By **Romell Tukes**

QUIET MONEY III

THUG LIFE II

By **Trai'Quan**

THE STREETS MADE ME III

By **Larry D. Wright**

THE ULTIMATE SACRIFICE VI

IF YOU CROSS ME ONCE II

ANGEL III

By **Anthony Fields**

FRIEND OR FOE III

By **Mimi**

SAVAGE STORMS II

By **Meesha**

BLOOD ON THE MONEY II

By J-Blunt

THE STREETS WILL NEVER CLOSE II

By K'ajji

NIGHTMARES OF A HUSTLA II

By King Dream

THE WIFEY I USED TO BE II

By Nicole Goosby

IN THE ARM OF HIS BOSS

By Jamila

Available Now

RESTRAINING ORDER **I & II**

By **CA$H & Coffee**

LOVE KNOWS NO BOUNDARIES **I II & III**

By **Coffee**

RAISED AS A GOON I, II, III & IV

BRED BY THE SLUMS I, II, III

BLAST FOR ME I & II

ROTTEN TO THE CORE I II III

A BRONX TALE I, II, III

DUFFEL BAG CARTEL I II III IV

HEARTLESS GOON I II III IV

A SAVAGE DOPEBOY I II

HEARTLESS GOON I II III

DRUG LORDS I II III

CUTTHROAT MAFIA I II

By **Ghost**

LAY IT DOWN **I & II**

LAST OF A DYING BREED

BLOOD STAINS OF A SHOTTA I & II III

By **Jamaica**

LOYAL TO THE GAME I II III

LIFE OF SIN I, II III

By **TJ & Jelissa**

BLOODY COMMAS I & II

SKI MASK CARTEL I II & III

KING OF NEW YORK I II,III IV V

RISE TO POWER I II III

COKE KINGS I II III IV

BORN HEARTLESS I II III IV

KING OF THE TRAP

By **T.J. Edwards**

IF LOVING HIM IS WRONG…I & II

LOVE ME EVEN WHEN IT HURTS I II III

By **Jelissa**

WHEN THE STREETS CLAP BACK I & II III

THE HEART OF A SAVAGE I II

By **Jibril Williams**

A DISTINGUISHED THUG STOLE MY HEART I II & III

LOVE SHOULDN'T HURT I II III IV

RENEGADE BOYS I II III IV

Romell Tukes

PAID IN KARMA I II III

SAVAGE STORMS

By **Meesha**

A GANGSTER'S CODE I &, II III

A GANGSTER'S SYN I II III

THE SAVAGE LIFE I II III

CHAINED TO THE STREETS I II III

BLOOD ON THE MONEY

By J-Blunt

PUSH IT TO THE LIMIT

By **Bre' Hayes**

BLOOD OF A BOSS **I, II, III, IV, V**

SHADOWS OF THE GAME

By **Askari**

THE STREETS BLEED MURDER **I, II & III**

THE HEART OF A GANGSTA I II& III

By **Jerry Jackson**

CUM FOR ME I II III IV V VI

An **LDP Erotica Collaboration**

BRIDE OF A HUSTLA **I II & II**

THE FETTI GIRLS **I, II& III**

CORRUPTED BY A GANGSTA I, II III, IV

BLINDED BY HIS LOVE

THE PRICE YOU PAY FOR LOVE

DOPE GIRL MAGIC I II III

By **Destiny Skai**

WHEN A GOOD GIRL GOES BAD

By **Adrienne**

THE COST OF LOYALTY I II III

By Kweli

184

A GANGSTER'S REVENGE **I II III & IV**

THE BOSS MAN'S DAUGHTERS I II III IV V

A SAVAGE LOVE **I & II**

BAE BELONGS TO ME I II

A HUSTLER'S DECEIT I, II, III

WHAT BAD BITCHES DO I, II, III

SOUL OF A MONSTER I II III

KILL ZONE

A DOPE BOY'S QUEEN I II

By **Aryanna**

A KINGPIN'S AMBITON

A KINGPIN'S AMBITION **II**

I MURDER FOR THE DOUGH

By **Ambitious**

TRUE SAVAGE I II III IV V VI

DOPE BOY MAGIC I, II, III

MIDNIGHT CARTEL I II

CITY OF KINGZ

By **Chris Green**

A DOPEBOY'S PRAYER

By **Eddie "Wolf" Lee**

THE KING CARTEL **I, II & III**

By **Frank Gresham**

THESE NIGGAS AIN'T LOYAL **I, II & III**

By **Nikki Tee**

GANGSTA SHYT **I II &III**

By **CATO**

THE ULTIMATE BETRAYAL

By **Phoenix**

BOSS'N UP **I , II & III**

Romell Tukes

By **Royal Nicole**
I LOVE YOU TO DEATH
By Destiny J
I RIDE FOR MY HITTA
I STILL RIDE FOR MY HITTA
By **Misty Holt**
LOVE & CHASIN' PAPER
By **Qay Crockett**
TO DIE IN VAIN
SINS OF A HUSTLA
By **ASAD**
BROOKLYN HUSTLAZ
By **Boogsy Morina**
BROOKLYN ON LOCK I & II
By **Sonovia**
GANGSTA CITY
By **Teddy Duke**
A DRUG KING AND HIS DIAMOND I & II III
A DOPEMAN'S RICHES
HER MAN, MINE'S TOO I, II
CASH MONEY HO'S
THE WIFEY I USED TO BE
By Nicole Goosby
TRAPHOUSE KING **I II & III**
KINGPIN KILLAZ I II III
STREET KINGS I II
PAID IN BLOOD **I II**
CARTEL KILLAZ I II III
DOPE GODS I II
By **Hood Rich**

LIPSTICK KILLAH **I, II, III**

CRIME OF PASSION I II & III

FRIEND OR FOE I II

By **Mimi**

STEADY MOBBN' **I, II, III**

THE STREETS STAINED MY SOUL

By **Marcellus Allen**

WHO SHOT YA **I, II, III**

SON OF A DOPE FIEND I II

Renta

GORILLAZ IN THE BAY **I II III IV**

TEARS OF A GANGSTA I II

3X KRAZY

DE'KARI

TRIGGADALE I II III

Elijah R. Freeman

GOD BLESS THE TRAPPERS I, II, III

THESE SCANDALOUS STREETS I, II, III

FEAR MY GANGSTA I, II, III IV, V

THESE STREETS DON'T LOVE NOBODY I, II

BURY ME A G I, II, III, IV, V

A GANGSTA'S EMPIRE I, II, III, IV

THE DOPEMAN'S BODYGAURD I II

THE REALEST KILLAZ I II

Tranay Adams

THE STREETS ARE CALLING

Duquie Wilson

MARRIED TO A BOSS... I II III

By Destiny Skai & Chris Green

KINGZ OF THE GAME I II III IV V

Playa Ray

SLAUGHTER GANG I II III

RUTHLESS HEART I II III

By Willie Slaughter

FUK SHYT

By Blakk Diamond

DON'T F#CK WITH MY HEART I II

By Linnea

ADDICTED TO THE DRAMA I II III

IN THE ARM OF HIS BOSS II

By Jamila

YAYO I II III

A SHOOTER'S AMBITION I II

By S. Allen

TRAP GOD I II

By Troublesome

FOREVER GANGSTA

GLOCKS ON SATIN SHEETS I II

By Adrian Dulan

TOE TAGZ I II III

By Ah'Million

KINGPIN DREAMS I II

By Paper Boi Rari

CONFESSIONS OF A GANGSTA I II

By Nicholas Lock

I'M NOTHING WITHOUT HIS LOVE

SINS OF A THUG

By Monet Dragun

CAUGHT UP IN THE LIFE I II III

By Robert Baptiste

Murda Season 3

NEW TO THE GAME I II III
By **Malik D. Rice**
LIFE OF A SAVAGE I II III
A GANGSTA'S QUR'AN I II
MURDA SEASON I II III
GANGLAND CARTEL I II
By **Romell Tukes**
LOYALTY AIN'T PROMISED I II
By **Keith Williams**
QUIET MONEY I II
THUG LIFE
By **Trai'Quan**
THE STREETS MADE ME I II
By **Larry D. Wright**
THE ULTIMATE SACRIFICE I, II, III, IV, V
KHADIFI
IF YOU CROSS ME ONCE
ANGEL I II
By **Anthony Fields**
THE LIFE OF A HOOD STAR
By **Ca$h & Rashia Wilson**
THE STREETS WILL NEVER CLOSE
By **K'ajji**
CREAM
By **Yolanda Moore**
NIGHTMARES OF A HUSTLA
By **King Dream**

Romell Tukes

<u>BOOKS BY LDP'S CEO, CA$H</u>

<u>TRUST IN NO MAN</u>
<u>TRUST IN NO MAN 2</u>
<u>TRUST IN NO MAN 3</u>
<u>BONDED BY BLOOD</u>
<u>SHORTY GOT A THUG</u>
<u>THUGS CRY</u>
<u>THUGS CRY 2</u>
<u>THUGS CRY 3</u>
<u>TRUST NO BITCH</u>
<u>TRUST NO BITCH 2</u>
<u>TRUST NO BITCH 3</u>
<u>TIL MY CASKET DROPS</u>
<u>RESTRAINING ORDER</u>
<u>RESTRAINING ORDER 2</u>
<u>IN LOVE WITH A CONVICT</u>
<u>LIFE OF A HOOD STAR</u>

Murda Season 3

9 781952 936647